to Betty and
John with
all my eore
Helen McClog

Boston,
December, 1968.

Mr . Splitfoot

Mr. Splitfoot

By HELEN McCLOY

DODD, MEAD & COMPANY

NEW YORK

In memoriam
For my cousin
Miriam Worrell Webb

"Do as I do, Mr. Splitfoot!"

KATIE FOX

Mr . Splitfoot

1

SHE WAS CAREFUL to avoid the one stair that creaked. As far as she knew, the house was empty, but . . .

You never could tell. They had said They were going skiing all afternoon, but They might come back at any moment.

They did as They pleased. They did things you would have been punished for doing, but there was no one to punish Them. They thought you didn't know what They did. But you did. Always.

They often said They felt just as if They were fifteen at fifty. Didn't They realize that you often felt just as if you were fifty at fifteen? At twenty-one you would be as free as They, but twenty-one was a long way to go, six whole years. Meanwhile . . .

On the second floor, she paused to listen. The house was still silent. Beyond the open window, the world was windless and leafless—just stony, skeletal trees, forking and branching in dark lung patterns against a dazzle of sunlit snow. The icy stillness seemed dead as the cold beyond galactic space where even molecular motion must cease and there is no such thing as time. . . .

It was sort of scary. More scary than dark of night for, in this brilliant light, you could believe that somewhere someone you couldn't see was watching you. Someone who approved what you were going to do. Someone . . . or Something . . .

She opened the second door on her right. The room was empty, as she had known it would be. She slipped inside, noiseless in stocking feet, and closed the door softly behind her. She stood with her back against the door, looking around the room. A slow smile curved her lips. This feeling of secrecy was exhilarating. I know something you don't know. Power.

White walls. A white ceiling with dark, exposed beams. Tall, printed curtains—violets and green leaves on a white ground. The counterpane was white, the quilt, violet satin with the pearly lustre of real silk. There were little ash trays and pin trays of French porcelain, violet figures on a white ground. Trust Folly to think of the smallest detail. Even the carpet was another shade of the same violet, . . . plummy velvet, accented by a hearth rug of white fur, and the old tiles around the grate were faded mauve and oyster-white. There were bits of copper and purplish lusterware on the chimney shelf, and the highboy was rosewood.

Again she smiled. There were all kinds of things you could do in a room like this. You could smash the lusterware. You could throw ink on the white fur. If you had a sharp knife, you could slash the curtains and score the tiles and rip up the carpet. If you lit a fire, you could burn those old books in the bookcase. What a stench the leather bindings would make. . . .

But these were things that would make Them angry, and you didn't want to make Them angry. You wanted to make Them afraid.

If They were really afraid, They wouldn't think of punish-

2

ing you, because it would never occur to Them that you were responsible. They wouldn't think you bold enough, or cunning enough, to frighten Them.

You would have to be exquisitely subtle. One thing at a time. A little hint here, a little coincidence there. Things that couldn't quite be explained according to any of Their rules. After a while the cumulative effect would get under Their skins. Gently, quietly, almost imperceptibly, you could undermine Their deepest faith—Their faith in Themselves. Then you would have Them at your mercy.

What would be the best beginning?

Her favorite case was the Portuguese villa at Coimbra in 1919. Unfortunately she had no idea how to duplicate the things that had happened there. That was what made the case so fascinating. Assume the thing was a hoax: you still had a mystery. How were those effects contrived?

So she would have to fall back on something else. The Norman castle at Calvados in 1875? Even then she would have to stick to the simpler incidents. No one had ever been able to explain some of the others. . . .

A snapping sound cracked the silence. There was a floor board in the upper hall that creaked when you stepped on it. Could They be back already? She stood still, breathless, waiting. No other sound came.

She counted to sixty seconds slowly. One-and, two-and, three-and . . . Still no further sound. She must have been mistaken. Or the temperature outside was changing and the old house was resettling itself for the night on its arthritic foundations. . . .

She crossed to the highboy, opened the top drawer. A jewel case, a handkerchief box, a glove box. She shut that drawer and opened the next. Ah! That was better. Stockings.

They had been washed and dried and rolled in pairs and the sheerest put away in a violet satin bag scented with lavender. She took out twelve pairs. Six were dust-gray beige, three were sheer black, and three an odd smoky shade of blue. The latest thing. She walked over to the bed. Swiftly she arranged them in the pattern of a large figure eight, then stood back to contemplate the effect.

Did it seem uncanny to her only because she knew about the others things that had happened at Calvados at the same time? They didn't know about those things. To Them, this would be just a silly trick . . .

Unless she could make Them believe the house was empty when it happened? But how could she make Them believe that?

"Caught you!"

Lucinda jumped as if a firecracker had exploded. In the looking-glass above the highboy, she could see the half-open door. Vanya was standing in the doorway. It would be Vanya, of course. None of Them would ever sneak up on her like that.

"I heard you!" she cried. "I heard the floor board in the hall creak!"

He was grinning. "No, you didn't, because I didn't come along the hall. I came up the stairs."

"Then what did I hear?"

"Old beams groaning. It's getting colder outside." He was looking at the figure eight on the bed. "What the hell? Oh, I get it. The Norman castle. But you oughtn't to start with that, Worm."

"I wish you wouldn't call me 'Worm'!"

"Why not? You look like a worm. One of the white ones you find under damp stones."

"Thanks a lot! You'd better remember that worms turn."

"I don't think you ever will."

"Perhaps I'm turning now."

"Oh?" His gaze went back to the stockings. "But not

4

against me. Against her. Folly. This is her room, isn't it?"

"Yes."

"You should start with something more punchy and use the figure eight later, when tension has built up to a point where even the silliest things are terrifying."

"I suppose you're going to tell on me now and spoil everything!" She was always on the defensive in his presence, for he made her aware of all her shortcomings. She was painfully thin and flat-chested for her age and sex. Strangers mistook her for twelve rather than fifteen. Her colorless face was spattered too generously with freckles. Her eyes were a dull gray; her hair what Folly called "hair-colored hair," straight and lank. She was conscious of all this when she looked at Vanya, because he was the handsomest boy she had ever seen.

It wasn't his height or his bold profile and shock of black hair. It was his eyes, the dark, deep-set eyes that reflected every mood so instantly. How quickly the warm glow of affection could turn into the hard flash of anger or the bright spark of mischief. When he was angry, his eyes got round under drawn brows and he looked like a caged eagle. At the moment his mood was high mischief, and the sparks were dancing.

"I wouldn't think of spoiling this. I'm going to help."

"Oh, Vanya!" For a moment she almost loved him.

"It takes two to do this sort of thing. You wouldn't have a chance alone, but the two of us together . . . Before the week is out, we'll have them calling the police."

"Or the Society for Psychical Research."

He looked at her with new respect. "That's even better. You do have ideas. I wonder if we could get Them that scared?"

"I don't see why not." His praise made her bolder.

"They're always frightened by anything They can't ex-

5

plain. That's why They invented Science—to make the universe safe for Them by hiding or ignoring anything that can't be explained according to Their rules."

"Sweeping the dirt under the rug? You're right, of course. If we can make Them consider, just once, only for a moment, that reality is incoherent and unintelligible, They'll flip . . . Put those stockings back."

"Then what?"

"We must think this out carefully." Vanya sat down on the fur rug, cross-legged, his brow ridged in deepest thought. Lucinda perched on the edge of the bed and waited. Beyond the window, the western sky was banded with primrose light that made shadows on the snow look blue.

At last the oracle spoke. "Could you manage the traditional smell of violets?"

"Sure. Folly has some stuff called April Violets."

"Then . . . I'm tempted to try the trick that was used in the Reverend Dr. Eliakim Phelps' parsonage in Connecticut in 1850."

"The tableau? At Stratford?" She was as familiar with the literature as he. They had studied it together all last summer.

"I always liked that one." He began to intone dreamily: *"Eleven bizarre dummies, constructed out of the family's clothing, arranged in attitudes of prayer with open Bibles before them."*

"All females except for one ugly, male dwarf . . . What was it Dr. Webster said?"

"It wouldn't have been possible for half a dozen women working several hours to have completed their design, yet these things happened in a short time with the whole household on watch."

"And they were so lifelike a small child thought his mother

6

was kneeling with the rest . . . Vanya, you and I couldn't manage anything like that."

"I know. Besides, there's more shock value in sound effects. Our first attack must be a real assault on the nervous system."

"How do we go about that?"

"The poltergeist bit. Knocking, rapping. What time is dinner tonight?"

"Eight o'clock."

"How long does it take?"

"About an hour."

"They don't sit around the table drinking brandy after dinner or any of that nonsense, do They?"

"No, if They want brandy after dinner, They have it in the living room with coffee."

"Good. Then we'll time this for half-past nine. That gives us a margin of thirty minutes if They should talk a lot or dawdle over their food."

"Time what?"

"The raps in the living room. They'll make the usual remarks about water pipes and heating systems and beams contracting as it gets colder after sunset. And then you'll say . . ." Vanya's voice became falsetto. *"Isn't there a tradition that this house is supposed to be haunted?"*

"I can't say that."

"Why not?"

"I'm not supposed to know. I overheard Folly telling the gardener not to mention it to me last summer."

"She's a goop if she thinks she can keep a thing like that from you. Does she suppose you don't know why that room at the head of the stairs is never used?"

"I told you she was a goop."

"All right. You don't have to say anything about the house

7

being haunted. They'll remember."

"They may not. My father doesn't believe in that sort of thing."

"But your mother does."

"Stepmother, and she does not!"

"She does so! I've overheard her and your father talking and—"

"How could you overhear them? Where were you listening?"

"None of your business."

Lucinda considered him thoughtfully. "Am I supposed to say anything else? After the knockings begin?"

"Oh, yes." Again Vanya's voice climbed to a falsetto. *"I've just noticed something funny. Those knocks are all coming in groups of three* . . . Then They'll tell you it's just your imagination, and They'll laugh to show how skeptical They are, but the laughter will be a bit thin and then . . . Do you know what you'll do then?"

"No. What?"

"You'll do just what Katie Fox did."

"Ooooh!" For a moment Lucinda's eyes were as brilliant as Vanya's and she was almost pretty.

He smiled. "So you remember?"

"Oh, yes! Who could ever forget? I'll cry out, very loud: 'DO AS I DO, MR. SPLITFOOT!' And I'll clap my hands three times and there'll be three knocks in response and then They'll stop talking about beams and pipes, because beams and pipes can't count to five . . . But, oh, Vanya, how can we manage to do such a thing?"

"Easy as pie. I'll be making the knocks."

"They'll search the house. They'll find you."

"They may search the house, but they won't find me."

"Why not?"

"That's my secret and I'm not going to tell you."

2

THIS SNOW HAD never been told that large flakes are the sign of a brief flurry. These flakes were large, but they had been falling for three hours and they were still at it. It was not so bad in the Hudson River valley, but when the car left Saugerties and began to climb into the mountains at Palenville, the road became almost impassable.

In the valley the snow had fallen like powder on a dry surface. Here, in the mountains, it was falling on a crust of older snow that had melted to water yesterday and turned to ice tonight. Even snow tires had no traction. This was like driving on greased glass.

Basil Willing became aware that both his hands were clamped to the steering wheel. Deliberately he loosened his fingers and flexed them, but tension was still in his heart. There was nothing he could do about that.

The headlights showed only the tops of pine trees below him on his left, but he knew that the darkness beyond hid a drop of five hundred feet or more only a few inches from the edge of the steep, twisting road. He also knew that the car might skid at any moment.

"Bad?" The voice of Gisela, his wife, was a cool sweetness.

"Very bad. I'm going to get off this road the first chance I have."

They were descending now and there was a curve. The car gave a giddy lurch and spun a foot or so clockwise, but did not leave the road. Rotating headlights came to rest on a rocky height above them on their right. In summer there would be a waterfall there. Now the crags were bearded with great icicles. The engine died and the car stood directly across the road, blocking the way like a barricade.

"At least there's no traffic," said Gisela.

"No one but us would be fool enough to be out here on a night like this. I sometimes wonder if skiing is worth it."

Gisela laughed. "Perhaps we should just abandon the car and put on our skis now. Much safer."

Basil started the engine gingerly and gently coaxed the car to turn its nose in the right direction. Now they were climbing again. Was there no end to these mountains? They couldn't leave the road on the left for there was the drop below them, and they couldn't leave the road on the right for there was the rocky height above them. There were no stars, no moon. All they could see was a mad tarantella of windy snowflakes in the restricted glare of their own lights.

"Like a white curtain," said Gisela.

"But a curtain made up of moving particles," added Basil. "The way most people imagine the dance of the electrons inside the atom."

"And it's not really that way?"

"Of course not. There are astronomical spaces between electrons and then there's the fascinating question of whether they really exist at all."

He was talking at random to keep her mind off the road.

"But they do, don't they?"

"Do they?" As he couldn't take his eyes off the road, he tried to put the smile into his voice. "When a thing is so

10

elusive that you can't determine its velocity and position at the same time—"

"Basil! A side road!"

The headlights picked out a narrow, winding track that tunneled into the woods on their right.

"Thank God!" He turned the car into what must be a leafy lane in summer.

"But we don't know where it goes!"

"I don't care where it goes, so long as we get away from those cliffs. If we skid here, the worst thing that can happen is that we wrap the car around a tree. At this speed it won't hurt us—only the car."

"I thought some of the worst accidents occurred at low speeds."

"This isn't a speed. It's a slow. We're crawling."

They were on relatively level ground here. They rounded one curve and another and another. "Have you any idea where we are?" Gisela asked him at last.

"Not the faintest. We'll have to stop at the first house and ask for directions."

"But there don't seem to be any houses on this road."

"There must be. A road has to lead somewhere. People don't build them just for fun."

"Perhaps we're passing houses without seeing them because they have no lights."

"At eight o'clock in the evening? Even in the mountains people don't go to bed that early. Not since the invention of television."

"What about summer cottages, closed for the winter?"

"Would the county build a whole road just for summer cottages?"

"It may be a private road, a dead end."

"If it is and all the houses are closed, we'll just have to turn back. But let's hope we come to a house or another road in a few more minutes."

He knew vaguely that they must be on top of the mountain now where it leveled off into a sort of plateau furrowed with shallow valleys and ravines, but after so many twists and turns, he had lost all sense of direction. If only there had been stars! He felt as lost as a child playing blindman's buff.

The snow was deeper now. There was a theory that you should drive in high gear on deep snow, but the way was growing so steep again that he decided to shift into second. A mistake. There was an ominous clonk and the engine died. He turned the ignition to "start." The engine muttered with just the sound of a human voice swearing under its breath, so you couldn't quite catch the words. He stepped on the gas. The engine went on muttering, but the car didn't move. He tried again. The muttering was slower. It died and silence enfolded them.

He looked at his wife. "Transmission, probably. Job for a garage. Several days and at least a hundred dollars. Were you joking about putting on our skis? It's not a joke now. We must ski or walk."

They were dressed for the weather—insulated underwear, heavy ski sweaters, wool slacks and fur-lined parkas. They got into ski boots and adjusted skis by the light of the headlamps. He glanced at Gisela before he switched off the lights. In those clothes she looked like a boy until you noticed the fine cut of her profile and something essentially feminine in the depth of her dark eyes.

"You and I have been in worse situations than this," he reminded her.

"I know." They exchanged the most intimate of all smiles, the smile of shared memory. "I suppose we should keep to the road. As you said, a road has to lead somewhere."

"Except in dreams."

"But this isn't a dream. It's reality. Remember?"

12

"Is it? I'm not so sure . . . Look! Lights. I don't quite believe in them, do you? Too pat. A moment ago we were miles from anywhere."

They had glided downhill and around the next curve. Now they were standing at the top of another hill. Below them, on the floor of a wide valley, stood a house with brilliantly lighted windows.

"How beautiful!" Gisela breathed softly. "Like coming suddenly on a lighted ship at sea."

"Or a Japanese house."

"Because it's broad and low and sitting among terraces and gardens with trees just beyond?"

"Partly, but it's more the way the roof is shaped and placed in relation to the low lines of the house. Somehow those lighted windows look like *chosi* screens, and the whole thing seems frail and impermanent."

"To me it looks more like a toy Noah's ark, a boat on a platform."

"But the roof is almost Chinese. You expect the corners to curve up and then they don't."

"An odd house."

"And, therefore, an old house. Today builders use standard blueprints and houses look alike."

"I wonder what kind of people live there?"

"Let's find out."

As they drew nearer, it seemed less odd and Oriental, but it was certainly old. No picture windows. Casements with leaded, glass panes. And the level spaces muffled in snow weren't terraces. They were verandas without roofs.

"I think there are steps under the snow—" Basil turned his head as he spoke to her, but she wasn't there.

"Gisela!"

"I'm all right." She had fallen into a drift; only her head and shoulders rose above it. "All but my ankle. It turned

13

right over."

"Try to stand." He helped her into an upright position. She leaned on him heavily. "Will it bear weight?"

"Not comfortably. Probably a sprain."

He unlaced the ski boot. His knowledgeable fingertips explored the ankle. "I suspect something more serious. Probably an inversion fracture."

"Is that bad?"

"Not really, but you mustn't walk much until I can get you into a cast."

"But I have to walk! At least to the house."

"No, you don't. Wait here a few moments."

He groped his way through the snow to the veranda steps alone. He could hear a murmur of voices from inside the house. There was no bell beside the front door, but there was a knocker of wrought iron. "It would be brass on a new house," he thought as he knocked.

The murmur of voices stopped and he heard footsteps. He had been standing away from the windows in darkness. Now he was suddenly bathed in the glare of two carriage lamps on either side of the front door. They made everything look like a scene on the stage: snow falling through spotlights; one magnificent tree in the foreground, its trunk of dark, wet-looking *papier-maché,* stippled with paint that looked like pale, lacy lichen; beyond, a suggestion of tall pine trunks rising into a shadowy confusion of branches far above. Whoever painted that backdrop was truly an artist.

Half the wide door was swinging open, like a casement window. It was a New York Dutch door, derived, perhaps, from the European barn door. A man faced Basil in the opening. His once-blond hair looked cream-colored now it was turning white, but his face was that of a man in his late forties. He wore a sweater almost the same color as his hair, one of those Irish fisherman's sweaters that look as if they

14

were ivory carved in low relief. His sun-tanned skin had a golden tone. His eyes were like china tea, tawny amber, wide-spaced under level brows. The eyes and brows made him handsome, even in middle age.

"I'm sorry to have to bother you," said Basil. "But our car has broken down and we have no idea where we are. If we could telephone to a garage—"

The man's laugh had the rich tone of golden bells. "Are you kidding? It's all you can do here to get garage men out on a summer day, but on a night like this—"

Basil tightened his grip on his temper. "My wife has hurt her ankle rather badly. If there's any sort of motel or boarding house near here—"

"There isn't. The nearest is a good twenty miles, over by the ski lodge. You'd have to go back to Palenville to reach it by car. Tonight you could hardly take a trail over the mountain and walk!"

The thought of Gisela waiting in the snow put an edge on Basil's voice. "My wife cannot walk. Her ankle is broken. If we could borrow a car from you . . ."

The amber eyes went beyond Basil to the snow, still falling steadily. "You'd get stuck long before you reached Palenville."

"Francis! There's only one thing to do. They must spend the night here."

A woman had come to stand beyond the man's shoulder. She was tall and slender and blonde. The bone structure of her face had the symmetry of classical Hellenic sculpture and was as sexless. Take away Aphrodite's breasts and chignon and she is Hermes. She seems to derive as obviously from boy models as Shakespeare's heroines from boy actors. She has the wide waist, narrow pelvis and flat buttocks of a young male athlete. Her straight nose, round, beardless chin and sensual mouth are common to statues of both sexes and may be artistic conventions of the period. Whatever the cause, it is an epicene convention. There is nothing about face or figure that suggests the older mother goddess of earlier images who is so very much a functioning mammalian female.

The woman who stood behind the man in the doorway was as the figures in ancient marble and as cold. Her masculine aspect was emphasized by a slack suit of gray flannel cut to perfection by some master tailor. Immaculate white linen shirt, glossy, chestnut loafers, no jewels, no make-up. Utter self-confidence was all about her like a scent in the air.

The man turned his head to look back at her. Basil caught the look. Here was one man who did not find her cold. Her husband?

His eyes came back to Basil. "I'm sorry. We have a house party here and all the bedrooms are in use. Perhaps if I drive you myself—"

"A car will get stuck tonight no matter who's driving!" The woman's voice was beautiful, too. Low pitch, clean enunciation, and richly various tones suggested training. Actress? "There's only one thing to do. We'll ask them to camp out in the living room just for the night."

The man turned to Basil again with forced courtesy. "I'm afraid that's the best we can do. Where is your wife? Can I help you get her up to the house?"

"No, thanks. I can manage. And I am grateful for this."

Basil went down the steps.

"We're miles from a motel or a garage," he told Gisela as he unlaced her other ski boot. "We'll have to stay here overnight and hope to get you to a hospital the first thing in the morning. This ankle must be X-rayed."

Something in his voice caught her attention. "Did they invite us to stay the night?"

"Not with any great enthusiasm. I doubt if the husband believed your ankle was broken, but the wife did, and she

16

insisted. It won't be too comfortable. A couch in the living room. They have a house party and no bedrooms are free."

"A couch in the living room sounds wonderful."

He slid one arm under her knees, the other around her shoulders, and rose. She clung to his neck. "Quite sure I'm not getting too heavy for this sort of thing?"

"Not you! You haven't gained an ounce in twenty years."

The man held the door open for them. For the first time he was smiling. "Welcome to Crow's Flight! I must have seemed inhospitable just now, but we are a bit crowded this weekend. By the way, I'm Francis Swayne and this is my wife Folly."

Aphrodite smiled her marble smile.

Basil had a swift impression of a wide, tall room, paneled in unpainted wood, and a great, stone chimney. He put Gisela down gently on a sofa before a broad, open hearth. There was a fire. Its flicker kept shadows moving in the far corners of the room.

There were Christmas decorations everywhere—mistletoe overhead, a blue spruce tree glowing with blue lights, della Robbia wreaths that mingled winter fruit with evergreen branches and his own favorite—angel chimes from Sweden. The vanes of thin brass were highly polished, the candles below, whose updraft would send them spinning, were waiting to be lighted, and the little brass cherubs, that would revolve and strike thin notes from the chimes with slender rods, were poised and ready.

For a moment Basil thought that the bird cage shaped like a pagoda and painted white was part of the Christmas scene, but there was a flash of turquoise and white in the cage and a harsh voice spoke in grotesque parody of the human voice, breaking words up into syllables and running all syllables together.

"My-wife-Fol-ly!"

17

"Oh, be quiet, Tobermory!"

Gisela smiled. "Is he really like the cat in Saki's story?"

"No, he's just an echo. He has no idea of the meaning of what he says, though there are disconcerting moments when he seems to. That's why we named him Tobermory, of course."

"Francis Swayne . . ." Basil repeated. "The novelist?"

"I write novels." The tone implied: *And I don't like to talk about them.*

It was an attitude Basil had met in other writers and this time it was a relief, for he had never read a Swayne novel. Swayne was one of those novelists who had come out of the Pacific theatre of war and mined the rich vein of Far Eastern violence and mysticism for years afterward. Possibly Basil had avoided the novels because he had been in the Pacific theatre himself and preferred to keep his own vision of the Far East intact. Now that he saw the unusual qualities in Swayne's face, he was a little sorry he had done so.

"And this is a neighbor of ours," went on Swayne. "Ivan Radanine."

A boy had come forward to stand beside the Swaynes, a dark boy with a face as sharp as a knife. He was dressed for outdoors in thick boots and slacks and parka, but the heavy clothes did not clog his swift grace.

"My name is Basil Willing and this is my wife."

"How do you do, Dr. Willing?" The boy showed all his teeth in a wolfish grin.

Now how did he know that I was Dr. Willing?

"I'm sorry I have to go just as you arrive," went on the boy. "But I hope I may see you tomorrow."

"Not staying for dinner, Vanya?" Swayne seemed surprised.

"Thank you, but Mother insists I spend at least one evening a week at home, and this is it. Good night, Mrs.

Swayne . . . Dr. Willing."

A chilly blast came from the open door as he went out. Before it closed, Basil saw his own tracks in the snow filling rapidly with the falling flakes.

He turned back to Swayne. "I really can't thank you enough for putting us up. It's no night to be out in the mountains with a broken ankle and a balky car."

"Not at all. I'm just sorry we don't have an empty bedroom to offer you."

He checked himself suddenly as he saw another, older woman standing in the doorway to the right of the fireplace. Eyes still lovely looked out of the ruins of a once-lovely face. She was one of those women who always seem to be in motion—a shimmering scarf, a floating sash, a flutter of lace or pleats—and all her motions had poetry.

"Oh, Ginevra!" cried Swayne. "I didn't realize you had come down."

"I've been here several minutes." Ginevra's voice was soft, lilting, almost caressing. For a moment Basil couldn't place it and then it came to him. Irish. Not a brogue. Nothing so obvious. A cadence. Dublin University Irish.

"What are you talking about, Francis?" went on Ginevra. "You know perfectly well there's an empty bedroom at the head of the stairs. What's wrong with that?"

3

Lucinda stood alone in the upper hall at the head of the stairs. She couldn't see the lower hall, for the broad stair turned on itself, two flights joined by two landings, but she could hear sounds from the living room below.

She heard Vanya's demure *Good night, Mrs. Swayne,* and smiled. If Folly had any idea what a devil he was . . .

She heard a murmur that sounded like men's voices and then, suddenly, a woman's voice, soft and lilting: *You know perfectly well there's an empty bedroom at the head of the stairs* . . . That was the old one. Mrs. Alcott. The one They called Ginevra. She had really put Daddy on the spot now. It would be fun to hear him wriggle out of that one, but it would be more fun to use the few minutes exploring the upper floor now that she knew Vanya had some sort of secret hiding place here.

Vanya had gone. Daddy and Folly and Ginevra Alcott were all downstairs with these new people, the Willings. Only Mrs. Alcott's husband was left upstairs in his room. Probably getting out of soggy slacks and damp parka and into one of the odd outfits They called *après-ski.* He was old and slow and the others seemed quite occupied with one another down there. She could probably count on ten minutes without interruption. Perhaps fifteen.

They may search the house, but they won't find me . . . That's my secret and I'm not going to tell you . . .

The words went round and round silently in the deepest recesses of her mind like shadows of the spoken words. That was the part of the mind Montaigne had described so vividly, where nothing is forbidden and everything is hidden from everyone else. Like many adolescent intellectuals, Lucinda spent most of her time in the delightful freedom of that private kingdom. It was there she had been weighing Vanya's words ever since he uttered them.

He must have a hiding place in the house known only to him. He must have found it exploring the house during the years it stood empty.

Since he obviously believed that raps he made in this hiding place would be heard in the living room tonight, it must be close to the living room. Since he planned to come back to it secretly while they were all at dinner, it must be a place he could reach without going through the dining room and kitchen. The big living room was the only other room on the ground floor, so Vanya's hiding place must be upstairs.

But where? All the bedrooms were occupied tonight except the one at the head of the stairs that was never occupied. He knew that and he knew it was always locked. Could he have got hold of a key? Or did he plan to hide somewhere in the upper hall?

Slowly she looked all around her. The hall was straight and wide, with hardly any furniture and no carpet, just scatter rugs. It didn't look as if it afforded any hiding place for a boy as tall as Vanya. The only light was coming from a sconce near the head of the stairs. It left the greater part of the hall in shadow.

The walls were faced with paneling, oak or chestnut, she

21

wasn't sure which. It had never been painted, and now it was almost black with accumulated varnish, like an old picture in oils.

At this end the floor rose in a sort of ramp, sloping against the walls on either side to a height of about two feet, ending against the wall at the end of the hall near the stairs. This ramp must be the ceiling of the second flight of stairs below, she decided. Funny she hadn't noticed it before, but then she had never before examined the upper hall with such an analytic eye.

Old houses remodeled, like this one, had all sorts of architectural oddities. Patching up an old house was like patching up an old dress. You had to contrive all sorts of compromises, and the result was often more curious than beautiful, for there was no unity of design. . . .

That ramp would make a good slide . . .

At fifteen, you can still step back and forth across the line between adolescence and childhood. Lucinda stepped back. With knees bent, clutching the wall and leaning forward, she walked up the ramp as if she were walking into a high wind. At the top she turned and, bracing her hands against either wall, lowered herself gingerly into a sitting position, her legs straight in front of her. It was going to make a perfect slide. She must point out the advantages of this discovery to Vanya.

She let go of the walls. The varnished surface was slippery. She didn't want to slide too fast. Both arms flashed out. She tried to break her speed by pressing each hand against either wall. The left wall was solid, but the right wall gave way.

Her right hand clutched air and she slid, faster and faster, to a painful bump at the root of the ramp. She looked back.

A panel in the right wall had opened under pressure, like a narrow door. She was looking through the opening into a shallow chamber on the wrong side of the wall, the side where there was no plaster, only rough laths nailed to posts or beams with crumbs of plaster in the slits between the laths so you knew there was plaster on the other side.

The wrong side of the wall . . . The words echoed silently through that Montaigne part of her mind where she held endless conversations with her various selves. Just the echo of the words gave her a wonderful behind-the-scenes feeling. *Life is a play,* said one of her other selves. *And the backstage part is much more interesting than the footlights part, where everybody is all dressed up and aware of an audience.* Often she argued bitterly with her other selves, but this time she was in hearty agreement.

Was this Vanya's secret? It must be. She had really stolen a march on him, but suppose one of Them happened to come along now and discovered the whole thing?

She scrambled up the ramp and plunged through the opening, pulling the panel shut behind her. Now let Them come!

She was in total darkness, but she had matches for cigarettes. Forbidden cigarettes smoked with one's head leaning out an open window so there would be no telltale odor of smoke. They were big kitchen matches that Vanya had taught her to light with one flick of her thumbnail last summer. She lit one now.

In the fluttering light she saw a ceiling of rough laths and beams that seemed as high above her head as a cathedral roof. There were skylights up there. Dark dusty glass directly above her reflected the small light. She was standing in a narrow well, with walls on four sides. The walls rose to about two feet above her head, while the roof itself was at least twenty, possibly thirty, feet above her. She began to climb.

It was easy. Rough boards nailed between the posts that supported the lath wall made a ladder. At the top she found herself in an attic almost as big as the house itself. There were beams to walk on. She knew enough about attics to know that if she stepped on the lath and plaster part between the beams, she might crash through the ceiling below, so she was careful. Vanya's secret was her secret now and she didn't want anyone else to know.

They didn't know yet. She was sure of that. How often had she heard Their high, airy voices: *Crow's Flight has charm. Parts of it are really old and the view is delightful, but there's one drawback: no storage space. Not even an attic! Seems odd in an old house, doesn't it?*

If They'd searched thoroughly, They would have found the place, but They hadn't cared enough to search thoroughly and, luckily, there were no unexplained windows outside to draw Their attention to it. From the ground you wouldn't see skylights among all those gables.

But why hadn't the Crowes told Daddy about the attic when he rented the house from them last spring? David Crowe and Daddy had been close friends for years. You didn't hide such things from a close friend. There was only one explanation: David Crowe didn't know about the attic himself. But how was that possible? The house had been in his family a long time. That was where it got the name—Crow's Flight.

When had David Crowe acquired the house? Only a year ago, just before Daddy rented it from him. He had never lived in the house himself. He had told Daddy he couldn't afford to keep it up. And who had the house before the Crowes? A distant cousin in her nineties who died last year. So it was possible that David Crowe didn't know about the attic. When people got into their nineties, anything could happen. She might have forgotten to tell him or she might not have thought it important. That must be it, one way or the other.

And that was wonderful, because it meant the secret was all

hers. Hers and Vanya's. This wonderful secret place, like the mind itself, where nothing was forbidden and everything was hidden from everyone else. Ali Baba could not have felt greater exaltation as he set out to explore the treasure cave.

There was treasure here, too. Things that could never have belonged to Folly or Daddy. Old things. A bird's-eye maple washstand with a marble top. A pitcher and bowl, slop jar and chamber pot of incongruously lovely china, rosebuds on white. Dresden? A bicycle with a large front wheel and a small back wheel. A little Winchester rifle with a stock of figured walnut polished to the glow of a horse chestnut. A set of miniature furniture for a child, painted white with little wreaths of forget-me-nots. What child had loved it long ago? Most fascinating of all were the small trunks with rounded lids that made one think of chubby, pot-bellied babies.

Stepping delicately on the beams between the laths, she moved to the nearest trunk. It wasn't locked, but the latches were rusty. She had lit three more matches and broken a nail before she pried the trunk open. The hinges creaked like a chalk pencil on a slate. The lid was lined with faded wall-paper, green on white, a landscape with figures like a *toile de Jouy* print. There was a smell of camphor and mildew, with a faint trace of lavender and something else—the smell of oldness.

She lifted out one dress after another, ankle-length dresses with leg-of-mutton sleeves, narrow waists and full skirts, all made for a rather small woman. Black tulle and jet. Pale pink silk with tiny black dots and a black velvet sash. Voile printed with faded pink roses and faintly blue ribbons on a white ground, Dresden china colors. A fur jacket. Didn't they used to call it a "sack" or was it a "sacque"? Even it had *leg o' mutton* sleeves. Real sealskin too. Where it had worn, the seams were copper-brown. Real sealskin wasn't dyed totally black in those days.

Next came the hats. A small hat—a toque?—all *coq* feathers, black and green and iridescent as an oil slick. Long kid gloves, yellowed white with mother of pearl buttons. A fan of wilted white feathers with ivory sticks shedding fluff as if the moths had been at it. A man's opera cloak, black broadcloth lined with white satin, softer than anything she had ever touched. Opera glasses, gold and white mother of pearl, with a long handle that opened and shut like a spyglass and tiny letters that read *Lemaire, Paris.* They were in a little bag of purple panne velvet softer even than the satin.

There were scarf pins for a man's Ascot tie and hatpins in pairs, the kind they used to use to skewer huge hats to pompadour and chignon, top-heavy confections of flowers and ribbons and straw, feathers and velvet and tulle. Hatpins with long, slender steel shafts and points so sharp they could go through layer after layer of felt and velvet and satin. They had quaintly ornamental handles—little flexible fish made of tiny overlapping gold plates, roses made of rose quartz, little elephants carved out of old ivory.

The next trunk was a disappointment. Just old letters and papers. Some of them were really old. A Commission from the Supreme Executive Council of the Commonwealth of Pennsylvania made out to Josiah Crowe, gentleman, as lieutenant of a Company of foot in the first Battalion of Militia, in the County of Philadelphia, dated May 1st, 1786, and signed B. Franklin.

Lucinda tossed it, and other stupid old things like it, to one side, until she came to something more promising—a love letter.

> *Dearest Amelia*
>> *You know that I love you, and only you. Though your father is so inalterably opposed . . .*

What was the date on this one?

19th May, 1863.

For the first time a sense of life's desperate futility moved through Lucinda's immature mind, like the chilly wind that comes before a storm. Whatever the outcome of that letter, "dearest Amelia" and "your father" and the writer were all dead now.

She dropped the paper and picked up another.

> *Tapking and Gennerich, grocers*
> *1 lb. butter* . . . . *.06*

Six cents for butter? What was the date here? Oh, *1904* . . .

Lucinda thrust her hand down again among the packets of yellowed envelopes.

"It's wonderful you were able to get here on such a dreadful night."

Lucinda froze. It was Folly's voice and the words had an uncanny clarity as if she were speaking directly into Lucinda's ear.

"I do hope you'll be comfortable in this room," went on Folly. "If there's anything you need, just let me know."

"Thanks. . . . We only just made it, you know. In another hour nobody will be able to get through." The harsh voice and slurred enunciation were unmistakable—Serena Crowe.

"You've done this room over charmingly. This rose rug with the pale blue walls is so—so French. Everything's just lovely. I know we'll be comfortable."

"I'm so glad you like it," went on Folly. "I just looked in to tell you that cocktails are at seven."

"We'll be ready. David is in the shower now . . ."

So both the Crowes were here, David and his wife. Lucinda

sighed. If only she had paid more attention when Folly was talking about a guest list for this weekend. They couldn't know about the attic. They just couldn't for, if they had, they would certainly have told Daddy, and yet . . . Suppose they did know? Perhaps she ought to warn Vanya before he came back tonight. But how could she? There would probably be people in the living room all evening, and the telephone was there. No other extension in this house . . .

A door closed. There was a click of heels. Folly walking on the parquet between the scatter rugs in the upper hall. The sound died away as she reached the staircase.

Another door opened and a man's voice spoke. David Crowe's voice. "Folly is looking well."

"You thought so? I thought she looked awful, but men never see how she really looks. She blinds them with her dazzling charm. Hasn't she made this room horrid? Imagine a rose rug with blue walls!"

"I think it's rather original. Contrast and all that."

"You have no taste either. Cocktails are at seven. She just stopped in to tell us."

"It's seven now."

"Then I'd better go down."

"You'll not go until I'm ready to go with you."

"Why not?"

"I suppose you think I don't know what's going on, but I do."

Lucinda crouched closer to the lath and plaster, motionless, ears straining. This was more fun than television, and something like it, only you couldn't see, just hear. Rather like having a microphone in a guest room. Could you hear what was said in the other bedrooms, too? What about the living room if its door into the hall were open? How long had Vanya been using this place? What a lot he must know about everybody in the house by this time. . . .

Below her, voices were growing louder.

"I don't know what you're talking about!"

"I think you do!"

"What absolute nonsense!"

"Serena, I've had just about as much of this as I can stand. I can see the way you look at him and the way he looks at you."

"Oh, for heaven's sake! You—you're insane! Keep your voice down. Someone might hear us."

"No one could possibly hear us in here," said David Crowe's voice. "The walls are too thick."

Lucinda smiled. Surely that proved neither one of them knew about the attic. She wouldn't have to warn Vanya, after all.

"I didn't want to come here this weekend." David Crowe was still speaking. "I knew how you'd behave if we did, but I couldn't think of any graceful way to get out of it."

"Is it so important to be graceful?"

"Not to you—obviously. To me, it is. Bradford Alcott is my boss; Francis Swayne one of my authors. I can't offend either one. So here we are and we must make the best of it. In other words, I shall not let you out of my sight for a moment."

"Oh, David, what has happened to us? It didn't used to be like this."

"I've wakened up. That's all. I now understand why the Arabs say a wise man never leaves his wife alone with another man for the time it takes to cook a soft-boiled egg."

"Really, David!"

"Serena, I'm warning you. If you look at him just once the way you did that last time in New York—"

"Are you nearly ready to go downstairs?"

"No. I'm going into the bathroom to shave now and I expect to find you still here when I come out. You're not going down alone. We're going together."

A door closed with force, not quite a slam. There was silence and then the wail of a radio: *Lo-o-ve . . . is a many-splendo-o-red . . . thi-ing . . .*

Lucinda blew out the match she was holding and lit another. She had only three left. She guarded the flame with her open palm as she moved carefully from beam to beam. She'd better bring a flashlight next time. She had no wish to start a fire here when everything was getting so interesting.

He . . . him . . . What a pity David Crowe hadn't mentioned any name! Perhaps if one watched Serena Crowe carefully during dinner, she might give herself away . . . *The way you look at him . . . That last time in New York . . .* Yes, it really did sound as if Serena Crowe would betray herself to a close observer . . . How many men would there be at dinner anyway?

Lucinda didn't really care about the Crowes at this time. She was like a naturalist observing strange animals in their natural state. She enjoyed observing the wretched creatures and the way they took their pathetic little affairs so seriously, but she had no desire to interfere.

That came later.

The match flame died as she came to the "well," her name for the shallow chamber that opened into the hall. In darkness she could feel her way down from crosspiece to crosspiece, just like feeling her way down a ladder.

Now she was at the bottom of the well. A faint line of light from the hall outlined the panel she had closed when she entered. She crouched beside it, listening. Not a sound.

The Crowes would be in their room still. Daddy and Folly were probably upstairs changing, too, in the separate rooms they occupied. Those strangers who had come in to ask for shelter were probably still in the living room and Ginevra Alcott with them. Where was her husband? Bathing or changing, no doubt. Would this be a good time to slip out into the hall without too great a risk of being seen? Or should she wait until everyone else had gone downstairs?

She counted to one hundred slowly. Still not a sound. Her demon told her to take a chance. Now!

She pushed open the panel, stepped onto the ramp, drew the panel shut without a sound. There was no knob or catch. You had to pull it shut by the edge of its molding. Once in place, there was no break or crack in the wall that showed from this side. Had it always been this way, a door without knob or catch? Or had there once been some sort of door handle that someone had removed?

She slid down the ramp and started toward the stairs.

4

BASIL LOOKED UP as a girl came into the living room. He saw a wan, narrow face, speckled like the egg of some wild bird, and a body that was all angular adolescence in a mini-skirt. A Modigliani consumptive? No, a Cranach Virgin. Her hair was pure Cranach—long, straight, thin, lank, falling almost to her waist. How Gothic fashions would have suited her! A long, vertical dress, tight sleeves, pointed toes, hair strained back from the high forehead with a single pearl or ruby held by a thin chain between the eyes like a Brahman caste mark.

The modern shift she was wearing hung straight from shoulder to hem, but, unlike the medieval shift, this was a "psychedelic" print—discordant colors, magenta, mustard and turquoise in a blurred pattern that created an optical illusion of writhing motion.

Francis Swayne and Folly had both gone upstairs and it seemed as if Basil ought to introduce Gisela and himself, but before he could find words, Ginevra Alcott spoke from the little seat built into the nook between the chimney and the hall door.

"This is Frank Swayne's daughter, Lucinda. Mrs. Willing. Dr. Willing."

Only the girl's eyes moved—gray-green eyes that slid away from Basil's gaze before the eyelids could drop. The recoil was automatic as a reflex. Why was she so evasive?

She spoke in a pale voice. "Dr. Willing? Dr. Basil Willing?"

"I'm flattered, but also surprised." He leaned forward to watch the play of expression on her face more closely. "You really do know my name!"

She sank to the hearth rug, seeming weightless as a falling leaf. She tossed her long hair, then smoothed it with one hand. Girls with hair as long and loose as that couldn't leave it alone. They were always fussing with it. She looked at the fire as she answered him: "Vanya and I read one of your books last summer."

"The boy who just left?"

"Yes."

So that was why the boy had said "Dr. Willing" so glibly. These weren't ordinary children. Not if they spent their summers reading books on criminal psychology.

"Vanya lives just up the road with his mother," went on Lucinda. "She has quite a library. He and I read a lot there last summer because They wouldn't let us go anywhere. There was an epidemic. Polio. Of course we'd been inoculated, but so were some of those who got polio. They weren't taking any chances."

He noticed her odd inflection when she said "They."

It sounded as if the word were capitalized. Her world seemed to be that of the primitive clansman, divided into We and They. He surmised that anyone over twenty-five was They.

"What other books did you read?" asked Gisela.

"Oh . . . all sorts." She wasn't practiced at evasion. She might as well have said: *I'm not telling.* She hurried on as if to divert Gisela and Basil from those other books. "That was an old one of yours. About 1938, I think. Something about psychopathology and politics."

A rustle of silk from the chimney nook where Ginevra was sitting filled the little pause.

"Lucinda, what's all this about a bedroom that's never used? Your father simply wouldn't talk about it."

The girl's eyes grew wary.

"Daddy thinks I'll never find out if people don't talk about it. That's silly, because I know already."

"Why doesn't he want you to know?"

"He thinks I'd be frightened. That's silly, too. It takes more than that to frighten me."

And yet you are afraid, thought Basil. *Of something . . .*

"How did you find out?"

"Vanya told me all about it when we first came here last Spring. That's something else that Daddy doesn't know."

"Don't you think you ought to tell him?" Gisela's voice sounded unusually gentle after Lucinda's thin, sharp tone. Her voice, like her body, was all angles.

"Why should I?"

"I have a daughter about your age. It would bother me if she didn't tell me things like that."

Lucinda laughed. "You mean lack of communication and all that? I don't think there's ever real communication between parents and children. I suppose I'll think differently if ever I have children of my own."

Ginevra wasn't interested in generalizations.

"What's the story, Lucinda? Your father would hardly say a thing."

Lucinda regarded the flames in the hearth. "Just how much did he tell you?"

"Me? Nothing. He told the Willings they'd have to spend the night in the living room because there was no empty bedroom. Naturally I reminded him that there was one at the head of the stairs. He answered quite brusquely: 'That bedroom is never used.' Before I could ask why, the Crowes arrived and I didn't have a chance to talk to your father again before they all went upstairs."

"He's never done that before," said Lucinda.

"Done what?"

"Told people they had to sleep in the living room because there was no empty bedroom when there was. Of course the situation has never come up before. The house has never been so full of people. Still . . . I wonder if he's beginning to believe it himself?"

"Believe what?"

"The story about the room. It's really not like him to believe a ghost story."

"Nobody believes in ghosts, but everybody is afraid of them," retorted Ginevra. "Like Madame du Deffand. Come on, Lucy! Give! Unless your father has actually forbidden you to talk about this."

"He's never mentioned it to me at all."

"I sometimes think all parents are crazy," said Ginevra. "What would be more likely to rouse any girl's curiosity than locking up a perfectly good bedroom and never using it, even when the house is full of guests? And not even talking about it!"

"I suppose there's only one explanation." Lucinda was pensive. "He really does believe the story himself sort of halfway. Like the polio last summer. He said: 'There's no danger. You've been inoculated.' But still he wouldn't let me go anywhere."

Ginevra sighed. "We're still waiting for that story, Lucy."

"Well, it started in 1870 and—"

"What started in 1870?"

Basil had never heard a more tired voice. A man was standing in the hall doorway where Ginevra had stood before. A certain familiar note in his voice as he spoke to Ginevra made it clear that he was her husband, though he looked much older. His disenchanted eyes were hardly in focus. They managed to suggest that there was hardly anything in life worth their focusing for. His lips parted silently now and then as if he were short of breath, but he gave no impression of haste or anxiety. The effect he produced was closer to exhaustion. Why breathe? Scarcely worth the effort, really . . .

There was arrogance in such impenetrable ennui. Every languid tone, every indolent gesture seemed to say: *I have already seen everything worth seeing, done everything worth doing, and met everyone worth meeting. Why should I bother with you?*

Basil wondered if he realized that a manner which so deliberately excluded the other inhabitants of this planet was hardly likely to endear him to the most promiscuously egalitarian generation the world has yet seen.

He was resigned, but to what? Not financial failure, apparently. The lichen-gray tweeds and everything else in his appearance suggested a carefully disciplined elegance. How odd that a man should take such pains to please the eye and then make no effort to please the heart.

"My husband, Bradford Alcott," said Ginevra, and Basil remembered that Alcott and Blair were Francis Swayne's publishers.

So he wasn't resigned to failure. He must be resigned to success, and perhaps that was harder to bear in old age. Failure can console itself with so many ifs . . . *If I had made more money . . . If I had married someone else . . .* But there are no consolations for success. *I did make money . . . I did marry the woman, or women, I wanted . . . And now . . . is this all?*

Basil's glance shifted to Ginevra. By firelight you had a

36

glimpse of what she must have been years ago when the silvery hair was dark and the withered cheek round and velvety as a peach. In this light you couldn't see the cobweb-fine wrinkles. Just the brilliance of heavy-lidded eyes, deep and dark as purple pansies, the fluent grace in every gesture, the elegance of the Edwardian tea gown, crystal-beaded lavender banded with fur dark as her eyes.

"Dr. Willing?" Alcott repeated Basil's name with a rising inflection of simulated interest that only emphasized the weariness at the back of his voice. "Aren't you a criminologist?"

"Forensic psychiatrist," said Basil. "I sometimes work with the district attorney's office in New York."

"I thought so." Alcott drifted to a chair and collapsed with a sigh. "You've been mixed up in some curious cases. Wasn't there one at Brereton School years ago?"

Ginevra Alcott pounced. "Brereton School? That funny business about Faustina Crayle? I remember that. I had a cousin, Beth Chae, who was there at the time. Brad! Dr. Willing is just the person to lay the ghost here!"

"I didn't know there was a ghost here." Words left Alcott's lips reluctantly as if there were not quite enough breath to send them on their way.

"Oh, darling, everyone knows that when a bedroom is locked up and never used, no matter how full the house is, there must be a ghost in it somewhere."

Before Alcott could respond, the hall doorway framed another figure. Her *après-ski* array was too luxurious for Basil's taste—black velvet slacks, white mink shirt, pearls twisted in her bleached and braided hair. Her eyes were dull as two opaque gray agates under shallow water. She had paused by a lamp on the central table. Its light thrust upward, painting shadows in all the wrong places, revealing lines that would not have been visible in kinder light, and more—fine threads of scar tissue at the corners of mouth, nose, eyes and ears.

This was not cosmetic face-lifting. The scars were too many and too conspicuous. They had been placed by necessity, not art. Her whole face was such a carefully reconstructed mask of flesh that it was impossible to tell her age or even guess how she had looked before the operation. The same result would have been produced whether the face had been smashed at sixteen or sixty.

"Ghost?" Her voice was high-pitched, abrasive. "Don't tell me this house is haunted! How absolutely crashing! How totally tripwise!"

Ginevra spoke sharply. "Serena, did you meet Dr. and Mrs. Willing when you came in?"

"I'm afraid we were in rather a rush to get upstairs. I'm Serena Crowe." She smiled vaguely in Gisela's direction.

Serena. The name her parents gave her? Or a name assumed in afterlife as more romantic than Mary or Jane or Susan? If so, she had chosen badly. There was nothing serene about her. She was as uneasy as a little animal who has wandered too far from the familiar part of the forest where it knew which predators to avoid. This suggested the secretary who had married the boss or the boss's son and found herself lonely in the alien environment.

Ginevra was making conversation rather laboriously.

"The Willings had an accident in the snow. Their car broke down and Mrs. Willing hurt her ankle, so they are spending the night. Frank said they'd have to sleep in the living room. I'm trying to find out why they can't have the bedroom at the head of the stairs. I know it's empty. Is there a ghost story? You ought to know. After all, Frank and Folly only lease this house. It still belongs to your husband, and it's been in his family a long time, hasn't it?"

"Yes, but you'll have to ask him about the ghost. I never

heard of it before."

"'He hasn't come down yet."

"But he has. He came down with me a moment ago."

"We haven't seen him."

"He must be here. David?"

Serena's eyes moved in a circular glance around the room. "Yes, darling?"

He came through the door from the hall as if he had been standing just outside it. Listening? He smiled. It was just as if someone had suddenly switched on an electric light with higher candlepower. Everything in the room seemed brighter, clearer, more stimulating. The dark eyes were dancing with gaiety. Yet, behind the smile, there were lines in the face that were anything but gay.

Basil looked back at Serena's dead eyes and wondered, as he so often wondered when he met married couples for the first time, what had brought two such dissimilar beings together in the first place.

"What is it, dear?"

"Can you answer Ginevra's question? Or didn't you hear it? She wants to know if there's a ghost at Crow's Flight."

"Crow's Flight?" echoed Basil.

"That's what this place is called." David Crowe smiled again. "Much better than Crow's Nest, don't you think?"

"Much better."

"I don't know the reason for the name of the house. I like to think that some one of us Crowes fled here in disgrace long ago and came cross-country as the crow flies."

"And the reason for the family name?" asked Ginevra.

"God knows! After all, surnames are pretty recent, historically speaking. There are dozens of English surnames that come from birds—Peacock, Dove, Hawke, Nightingale, Parrott, Drake, Partridge. Some scholars derive Swayne from Swan. There are thirty-four birds in Chaucer's *Parlement of*

39

Foules. All but four survive as surnames today. Crow comes in many forms—Corb, Corbett, Corbin, Crake, Coe. They all sound rather like its cry, that 'vois of care' which makes it a bird of ill omen."

"Don't be morbid!" said Ginevra briskly. "And don't divert me from my original question. Is there a ghost?"

"I've never lived in this house myself, so I don't know much about it, but I've heard . . . stories."

"About the bedroom at the head of the stairs?" persisted Ginevra.

"Yes. That room has been locked up for about fifty years."

"But why?"

"Oh, the usual sort of reason. Everyone who has ever slept in that room has been found dead in the morning."

5

THE DINING ROOM WAS obviously an addition to the original house and a conscious effort to get away from its spirit and style. Perhaps this was an old terrace that had been roofed and walled. That would explain why the floor was brick. Three of the walls were glass masked now by drawn curtains of unbleached, raw silk. The fourth wall had been used by some artist to paint a mystical landscape in the Chinese manner, all airy space with a few sharp, precise suggestions of reality: a mountain peak without a mountain, a tree branch without a tree, and, in the foreground, a little man in a little boat on water otherwise undefined, so little that the empty space all around him seemed supernaturally vast, a whisper of infinity.

The sideboard was an old Korean chest, black lacquer and brass, polished by centuries of use. Each brass was a different, abstract design, shaped inside the limits of an invisible square, with all the deceptively improvised dash of the best Chinese calligraphy.

"I bought it in Seoul in 1950," said Swayne, noticing Basil's appreciative glance. "I had the rest of the room designed as a setting for it last spring. It's the only architectural change I've made in the house."

"Rather an extensive change to make in a rented house," said Basil.

Swayne smiled. "I intend to buy it."

"In spite of the ghost?"

David Crowe was looking down the long table toward his host. "Sorry I talked about that. I didn't realize you were trying to make a secret of it."

Swayne smiled. "Trying is right. Apparently I did not succeed."

He looked at his daughter. Her blood rose to meet his glance, reddening throat, cheek and forehead.

It was a long time since Basil had seen a girl blush. The occasion for this blush seemed insufficient. She must be in a state of high tension. She hadn't spoken at all during dinner, but she had seemed remarkably watchful, especially of Serena Crowe.

Basil believed that the best thing for the girl now would be to drag the whole business out into the light of reason. This was in his mind when he asked bluntly: "How did these people in the room upstairs die?"

"No one knows." Crowe's glance down the table shifted to Basil, but it was so oblique at that angle Basil could not read his expression. "The poor devils couldn't tell anyone what happened. They were dead."

"And the doctors?"

"Oh, they said 'shock.' It's like 'virus.' A word that means: 'I-don't-know.' "

"How many died?"

"Three altogether."

"Oh . . . must we?" It was Folly's dramatic voice.

"Don't worry about me," said Lucinda. "I've heard most of it."

"Oh? In that case . . ." Folly sighed.

42

As if she had read Basil's thoughts about her masculinity, she had assumed extravagantly female dress for dinner—harem trousers of jade green taffeta and a velvet bolero of sapphire blue that exposed a girdle of sun-tanned skin at the waist, in the fashion of the moment. She was shod in gilt—little Turkish slippers that curled up at the toes. In her ears and on her fingers were superb pieces of acid green jade that were probably Korean, too. She looked like a romantic Victorian's daydream of an odalisque, Dulac or Loti, Manet or Flecker, the Near East without smells and hunger, blood and tears.

The fact that she was so obviously Occidental, tall and athletic and blonde with a classically handsome face more like a boy's than a woman's, was all part of the make-believe role she had elected to play.

"Better bring it all out into the open now," said Swayne. "Much better than making a mystery of it. *Pas de mystère, pas de culte.* Let David tell the story and then it will be forgotten by all of us in twenty-four hours. If he doesn't, we'll imagine a lot of things worse than the truth. Trust the human mind for that."

Crowe took a sip of white wine from the glass beside his plate and then sat back in his chair. "I'll have to start with the house. The oldest part of it was built in 1840. It was a farm then, but it was not occupied by people who were farmers and nothing else. Jonathan Crowe was a woolen manufacturer who later sold cloth to the Union armies for uniforms. The family were proud of the fact that he didn't make a fortune. The manufacturers who did sold shoddy cloth, and soldiers died of exposure because of it. But Jonathan made enough to live comfortably and he retired from active business in his fifties, as people liked to do in those days if they could. The farm was a hobby for his old age.

"He is the first of my forefathers whose letters and books

have come down to us, so he's more than just a name in the family Bible. He's a solid, three-dimensional figure with a character of his own. He was an original, rather ahead of his time. Before the Civil War, he helped runaway slaves escape to Canada by hiding them in the cellar during the day so they need travel only at night. That was called 'having a station on the underground railway.' He embraced the Darwinian theory when it was still a heresy. In the library you'll find the *Vestiges of Creation,* a book that anticipated Darwin and Wallace by a few years, with notes on the margin in his own hand. He seems to have been a man who embraced anything that was new. His was the first house in the county to have central heating, and he dabbled in what we now call parapsychology—what the nineteenth century called psychic research and the eighteenth century called mesmerism. It was he who gave this place its romantic name, Crow's Flight. Until then it had been known simply as the Crowe farm, or the Crowe place."

"Did he have a family?" asked Gisela.

"By the end of the Civil War, he was a widower with three daughters, who had rather odd names. I wonder if you can guess what they were?"

"Faith, Hope and Charity?" ventured Ginevra Alcott.

"Oh, no. I told you he was a heretic. He had quarreled with all the clergy in the neighborhood. I think it must have been in a spirit of defiance that Jonathan Crowe gave his three daughters Christian names that were hardly Christian— Clotho, Atropos and Lachesis."

"I might have known it!" Ginevra sighed ecstatically. "The Three Graces didn't have names, did they? But the Three Fates did, and we even have an idea what they looked like, if we can trust Michelangelo. Did these three play a fateful role in the Crowe family history?"

David Crowe looked at her thoughtfully across the table.

44

"You're careful to say fateful, not fatal. How odd that so many words derived from the word fate should imply death."

"Not odd at all," protested Folly. "Fate is the inescapable, love and death. When the Victorians said 'his fate,' they meant either 'his love' or 'his death.' Were these three girls concerned with love or death?"

"Both." Crowe paused to relish a sip of wine. "Atropos alone lived to a great old age. She held tight to her property and hoarded her money. Her heirs, who had expected to be men of means while they were still young, soon realized that they would have to scratch for a living all through middle age."

"And what happened to Clotho and Lachesis?" It was as near to a show of interest as Alcott had come all evening.

"There was a young man."

"There always is."

"He had studied medicine at the University of Paris, so he must have represented all that was cosmopolitan and romantic in their eyes. I remember hearing that he taught them to play the waltz from the new opera, *Traviata*. There's a portrait of him around somewhere. He was handsome in a swarthy, saturnine way, with a high forehead and proud eyes. Just the kind of face repressed young ladies fall in love with in any era. What a pity the human sexual instinct is so dependent on visual impressions, but then some biologists say that sight was originally a male secondary sexual trait."

"Which one fell in love with him?"

Crowe laughed. "Which would you expect?"

"The youngest," said Lucinda.

"The oldest," said Folly. "She had been waiting longest."

"They say middle children are the loneliest," put in Gisela.

"All three of them had been living alone with their father

45

ten miles from the nearest town for a number of years," mused Basil. "And there were no cars. Just horses."

"You win," said Crowe. "They all fell in love with him, of course. Enter Conflict, laughing."

"Did he choose one?"

"The youngest, Lachesis."

"Why didn't she marry him?"

"He died. He was the first to be found dead in the room we're talking about."

"What happened?"

"It was about a week before the wedding. His family lived in town. By 'town' I mean what was then the drowsy little Hudson River village of Pratt's Landing and what is now the thriving little Hudson River town of Prattsville. He rode over to spend the day and, I suppose, make plans for the wedding."

"Imagine riding over that mountain road!" said Basil.

"People did, just as they used to drive through the Swiss Alps by *diligence* when my mother was a child."

"Diligence?"

"An open carriage and a pair of horses in summer. There was a great deal of summer travel in these mountains in those days. After all, we're in the same line of country as Saratoga and the old Catskill Mountain House."

"Did it happen in summer?"

"No, October. That may or may not mean snow up here, but that time it did snow. Like the Willings, he hadn't expected to spend the night here, but the roads were becoming impassable, as they are tonight, so Jonathan Crowe showed him to the only vacant room—a little room at the head of the stairs. There was only a couch there because the Crowes had always used it as a sewing room. Of course there was no gas or electricity then, so Jonathan Crowe lighted his guest's way

46

with an oil lamp and left it on a little round table beside the couch.

"Next morning, when the sun didn't rouse the young guest for breakfast, a servant was sent to his room. He was still lying on the couch, apparently asleep. Only when the maid-servant approached him did she see that he was dead."

"Didn't they make any attempt to find out how he died?"

"This was 1870, about five years after the Civil War. Medical jurisprudence was in its infancy, especially in country districts where police procedure is still more easygoing than in the big cities. He hadn't been ill. There were no wounds or other marks of violence on his body. His heart had just stopped. So the verdict was: *Death from shock, cause unknown.*"

"Did they lock up the room after that?"

"No. In those days, when families lived in houses for several generations, a room where a death had occurred was just another room. Clotho, the eldest, had always had a room of her own. Atropos and Lachesis had always shared a room. But, within a few weeks of the young man's death, Lachesis asked her father if she could move into the room where the death had occurred, the room that had always been a sewing room until then."

"Wasn't that rather odd?"

"There was no other empty room. Sharing a room with a sister who had also been in love with the dead man may have had its drawbacks for the one he had chosen, the one who had really lost him. Or she may simply have wanted privacy. We know now that even animals become abnormal in over-crowded living quarters. Among civilized human beings privacy is a necessity. If you haven't one room where you can be alone at will, you are living in prison."

"Was there talk of a ghost then?"

47

"Apparently not . . . unless you count Lachesis' own words as they have come down to us by oral tradition. She is said to have said to someone: 'I am not afraid. How could I be afraid of Laurence?' Anyway, whatever her reason, she did move her few belongings into the sewing room."

"And she was found dead in the morning?"

"Of course. The whole shape of the story as we know it from later developments makes that inevitable."

Crowe had the full attention of his audience now. There was a whiff of brimstone about that second death. They all felt it. Even Bradford Alcott turned his lack-luster gaze on Crowe with something like interest.

"And that's when the ghost talk started?"

"Well . . . if the heart just stops beating and there's no apparent physical cause, you naturally begin to think in terms of other causes.

"All we actually know is that after a few weeks Atropos asked if she could share Clotho's room. She explained the request by saying that the room she had shared with Lachesis was becoming distasteful to her. She said that she was always expecting to see Lachesis there. She didn't say that she saw Lachesis, or even that she felt the invisible presence of Lachesis. She just said that she expected to see Lachesis. Lovely word in that context—expected."

"And this is the first hint of anything like that?"

"Like what?"

"Like . . . well . . . overwrought nerves? Things left unsaid?"

"Oh, yes. Even then on the surface Atropos simply wanted to leave the room she had shared wih Lachesis because of its tragic associations."

"And below the surface?"

"Isn't it significant that there was never any question of Atropos' occupying any of the other empty rooms in the

48

house? There were two guest rooms and, after her father died, his room was vacant, but there was never any question of her occupying any of those rooms. She asked specifically to share Clotho's room with Clotho, as if she were afraid to be alone, and she must have been quite insistent for Clotho to give up the privilege of having a room of her own for what she must have regarded as a sick fancy of her younger sister's."

"Perhaps Clotho was afraid to be alone, too."

"Perhaps. Whatever the reason, Clotho and Atropos shared a bedroom for thirty years while all the other bedrooms in the house remained empty except when there were guests. The room where Lachesis and her young man had died was never shown to guests. Its door was never unlocked, and the myth grew."

"Naturally," said Swayne. "The myth-making part of the mind abhors coincidence. There has to be an intelligible pattern of cause and effect or we lose the illusion that we can control our environment. When no rational pattern is discernible, we automatically invent an irrational pattern."

"The genesis of this one is pretty obvious then," said Crowe. "Was it just coincidence that the only two people who ever slept in that room were both found dead the next morning? There must be something in the room that makes people die if they sleep there. Since there is no apparent natural cause, there must be a supernatural cause."

"Exactly." Swayne grimaced. "Myths, like scandals, grow rapidly as if they had a life of their own borrowed from the living minds that entertain them so hospitably."

"This particular myth grew fast as a weed," continued Crowe. "By the time Clotho and Atropos were old women it had become a Gothic romance. All three sisters loved the young man. One of them had stolen into his room the night before he died, one of the two he didn't love. She had killed

49

him by threatening to kill herself. She knew his heart was weak. She knew or at least hoped the stress of such a scene would be too much for him."

"And who killed Lachesis, then?"

"The jealous sister who had killed the young man also killed Lachesis later and by the same method, frightening her to death."

"Don't tell us she had a weak heart, too!" exclaimed Folly.

"Oh, no, those were the days when women fainted or went into a decline and died of a broken heart at the drop of a hat. You didn't have to prove that a woman's heart was physically weak in order to make people believe she had been frightened to death."

"Which was the killer, according to the myth?" asked Basil. "Clotho or Atropos?"

"It had to be Atropos. She is the one of the Three Fates who cuts the thread of life. Clotho and Lachesis merely spin and draw out the thread as it grows. Michelangelo painted Atropos shears in hand with a face that makes the Mona Lisa's smile look as naive as a baby's first grin. Why else did Atropos fear to go on sleeping in the room she had shared with Lachesis? Why else did she 'expect' to 'see' Lachesis at any moment? Isn't the murderer's fear of the ghost of the murdered the most ancient of all fears? Why else was Atropos afraid even to sleep alone?"

"Did Clotho suspect?"

"Who can say? She did take Atropos into her own room to live. Would anyone voluntarily share a room with a murderer? The myth-makers say 'yes.' They say Clotho must have suspected but she didn't probe because she had loved the young man, too, and been as jealous of Lachesis as Atropos. Whatever the truth, both surviving sisters lived under a cloud for many years with no company but one another, sharing one small bedroom in a house where there were four other bedrooms and several maids' rooms."

"Intimate hostility." Ginevra shuddered. "Too grim to think about."

"And it lasted a long time. They were both old women when Clotho was found dead one morning."

"Not in the room at the head of the stairs!"

"Of course. The symmetry of the myth demands that. There were two stories. First, Atropos killed Clotho because Clotho finally discovered proof that Atropos was guilty. Second, Atropos betrayed herself to Clotho involuntarily and she was afraid to let Clotho go on living once Clotho knew. The wicked flee when no man pursueth."

"But how and why did Clotho get into a room that had been locked up for a whole generation?" demanded Basil.

"No one knows, really. Again there were stories."

"What kind of stories?"

"There's never been much traffic on the road that passes this house, but a man did drive along that road the night that Clotho died, a farmer on his way to the farmhouse where Vanya and his mother now live. It was after midnight, but he saw lights in the house here and he heard pounding and someone crying: 'Let me out! Oh, God, let me out!'"

"And he didn't stop?"

"Most people hate being involved in family quarrels. The farmer had been drinking, he was barely literate and he believed every word he had ever heard about a ghost at Crow's Flight. He was human. He hurried home as fast as he could."

"But he talked the next morning?"

"Oh, yes. That's human, too. He talked after Clotho's body was found and people whispered that Atropos had forced Clotho into the haunted room and locked the door from the outside, leaving her alone all night with the terror that had been accumulating for thirty years. Clotho was an old woman

51

by that time. It was too much for her."

"And Atropos escaped justice?"

"Yes—if there was justice to escape. This whole story may be a tissue of lies concocted to explain a few coincidences and three natural deaths. Atropos is in her nineties now, paralyzed and speechless in a sanitarium. When she finally dies, the house will come to me. I'll be free to sell it then. All my interests are in New York. A place like this is too large and too far out for me."

"It's just what we've been looking for," said Folly. "A comfortable country house with plenty of land and privacy where we can live all year round. A writer doesn't have to live in town. When we do go in for a few days, we can always stop at a hotel."

Basil looked at Swayne. "And the ghost doesn't bother you?"

"Not me."

"But you keep the room locked?"

"David insisted on that when he let us have the house, so I agreed. There are plenty of other rooms."

"Only sensible thing to do." Folly's hands fluttered over the silverware beside her plate as if she couldn't keep them still and yet had to rationalize their fluttering by pretending the knives and forks needed aligning more precisely. "If there's any possibility at all that people die in that room for some reason we cannot understand, how frightful to take a chance on such a possibility! I'd much rather be called superstitious than find a guest of mine dead there some morning. Let's have our coffee in the living room, shall we?"

The fire on the great stone hearth had died down to what Gisela called a "ruby mine," a mound of incandescent red embers with almost invisible blue flames playing on their surface.

Swayne heaved a birch log across the embers, took down a bellows from the wall and added its breath to the chimney draught.

Basil was watching Lucinda. Why did the child keep stealing glances at her wrist watch guardedly as if she hoped no one would notice what she was doing? Was she expecting a telephone call? She couldn't be expecting a visitor so late on a night like this . . .

He was putting his coffee cup down on a table when the motion was arrested by a sudden sound.

The birch log? He glanced at the grate, expecting to see a shower of sparks, but there was none. He looked at Lucinda again. She had dropped her eyelids. One hand lay in her lap, palm up, relaxed, but the other hand, half hidden in a fold of her skirt, was clenched in a tight fist.

The noise came again. This time it was different. Or did it merely sound different to him because he could no longer associate it with the fire? It was no longer a knock or a rap. It was sharper, more like the snap of castanets.

Serena was smiling. "These old houses with their wooden beams! If they warm up during the day, the wood will contract when they cool off after sunset and then it's pop, snap, crackle!"

"It wasn't really warm today," said Crowe.

"And that doesn't sound like wood contracting," added Alcott. "More like a steam radiator. How old is the heating system?"

"Pretty old. As I said, it was the first in the county. But it's hot air, not steam. Registers, not radiators. Funny how fashion comes full circle. Now we're back again to fitted carpets and hot-air furnaces. When I was a child, they were hopelessly old-hat and everybody was ripping them out."

The next noises were louder. Lucinda spoke suddenly in a

53

high taut voice. "Why . . . those raps are coming in groups of three!"

"There must be someone tapping at the door," Gisela's voice was calm as if she were trying to set Lucinda an example.

"I doubt it," said Swayne. "But I'll make sure."

He switched on floodlights before he opened the wide front door. Falling snow glittered a silent shower of diamond dust in the light. Beyond, the newly fallen snow lay unmarked and immaculate.

"Nobody there." He shut the door and switched off the outdoor lights.

"Did you think there would be?" Lucinda's voice climbed higher. "Did you?"

She had risen. Her face was fever-pink. Her pale eyes glittered like the snowflakes. Her high voice rang out crystal-hard, eldritch, compelling:

"Do as I do, Mr. Splitfoot!"

She clapped her hands three times.

Promptly the answer came: Rap . . . rap . . . rap . . .

Folly gasped aloud.

Swayne spoke sharply. "Lucinda, do you know what's happening?"

Basil thought he saw a flash of malice in Lucinda's glance, but the glance was for Folly, not for Swayne.

Before she could answer him, the telephone rang.

Swayne picked it up. "Yes? . . . Oh, too bad. . . . She's here. . . . You want to speak to her?" His eyes were troubled as he looked at his daughter. "For you."

"For . . . me?" Lucinda was short of breath.

"Your friend Vanya."

"Vanya . . . but . . . where is he?"

"At home, of course. Where else would he be? He's calling

to tell you that he can't come out tonight and—God!"

Lucinda had crumpled to the floor. Basil had trouble finding her pulse. When he did, it was thin and irregular. She wasn't shamming. She had fainted.

6

THE CLOCK ON THE chimney shelf was close to eleven. Fresh logs on the fire had not yet caught and the living room seemed cold. Basil Willing crossed its wide floor to the front door. At his touch floodlights sprang into being outside and he saw through windows on either side of the door that the snow had stopped falling. Now there was only an arctic stillness in the white world beyond the door. He should have no trouble getting Gisela to the hospital tomorrow.

"Dr. Willing!"

Basil turned. Francis Swayne was standing in the hall doorway. Now he came forward.

"There's been a change of plan. After what happened, my wife has decided to take Lucinda with her and she's put Mrs. Willing in Lucinda's room. It's a single room, so both you and I will have to camp out in the living room tonight. I hope you don't mind?"

"Of course not. Is Lucinda better?"

"Quieter. I suppose that's the sedative you gave her." Swayne hesitated. "Dr. Willing, what do you think happened?"

"I don't know."

"Did someone play a trick on us?"

"I'd have to know a lot more about all of you before I could answer that."

"What do you think about my daughter?"

No beating around the bush. No mumbling: this-is-a-social-occasion-but-would-you-mind—? Just a plain question. Basil liked that.

"Again I can't give you a useful answer without knowing more about the situation. All adolescents have a tendency toward instability, especially if they are disturbed by some pressure in their environment."

"And Lucinda is?"

"It's obvious that she's unhappy in her relation with her stepmother."

"Folly tries so hard."

"Perhaps that's the trouble. She has to try. Living in an old house with a rather hair-raising legend hasn't helped Lucinda. You've kept the legend alive by keeping that room locked. Wouldn't it be healthier to throw it open and use it?"

"I promised David I wouldn't."

"He'll release you. He's here and knows what's happening."

"Does he?" Swayne took a deep breath. "I don't. You say you don't. Why did Lucinda faint? She never did that before. Saying 'shock' doesn't explain it. What shocked her? The three raps that seemed to answer her challenge to Mr. Splitfoot?"

"No," said Basil. "She didn't faint when she heard the three raps. She fainted afterward when she got the telephone call from Vanya. Who is Mr. Splitfoot?"

They were interrupted by a clatter of footfalls on the stair. David Crowe and Bradford Alcott came into the room together.

"Who is Mr. Splitfoot?" Crowe laughed. "Who has a

cloven hoof? The Devil, of course! He's known as Mr. Split-foot in parts of York state. The little Fox sisters came from this part of the world. It was December, 1847, when their father, John D. Fox, moved his family to a house in Hydesville, Wayne County, New York, near Rochester. It was in March of 1848 that the children, Margaret, aged seven, and Katie, aged six, first heard rapping noises that had been noticed by a previous tenant.

"Katie did just what Lucinda did. She clapped her hands and cried out: 'Do as I do, Mr. Splitfoot!' He obliged just as he did with Lucinda tonight and modern spiritualism was born."

"So this was plagiarism?" Alcott was languidly amused.

"Lucinda is obviously familiar with the curious history of Katie Fox. It has some odd features, like the skeleton found in that house long afterward."

Alcott suppressed a yawn. "All fraud, wasn't it?"

"Who knows?" Crowe laughed. "Poltergeist phenomena are becoming psychologically respectable since the neo-Freudians have found that they are associated with puberty. They seem to feel that there must be some truth in anything that can be related to sex. Even orthodox science is turning up so many oddities today that a man has to be very stubborn or very ignorant to say of anything: *That's impossible!* Did you know that during the Cuban crisis night photographs were taken from the air of cigarette ends burning in the dark twenty-four hours after those cigarettes had been extinguished? If you can photograph the past, you can do anything."

"All this is beside the point." Swayne was impatient. "My daughter fainted tonight for the first time in her life. I don't want that to happen again. Any suggestions, Dr. Willing?"

"Only what I was just saying. This business of keeping a room locked up because of an old wives' tale is unhealthy.

The taboo should be broken as dramatically as possible. I suggest that you take the living-room couch tonight and let me sleep in the so-called haunted room."

Basil anticipated several possible reactions—relief that sleeping arrangements were made so easy, smiles at his mock-gravity when he used the word "haunted," magnanimous protest: *Oh, no, if anybody's going to risk it, I'll do it* . . .

The one thing he had not anticipated was the reaction he got—utter dismay.

Swayne spoke first. "We can't do that. If anything did happen . . . No. I can't risk it."

"You know there's no risk," insisted Basil. "We're destroying a legend. With luck, we might trap a trickster. Mr. Splitfoot. But we're not laying a ghost because there are no ghosts, except in the minds of the living."

"Has it occurred to you that the three deaths in that room may have been caused by some condition there that is perfectly natural?" suggested Alcott. "David, you said the house had the first central heating system in the county. Even today with the most modern systems gases can escape from faulty ducts, and so on. With an older system a thing like that is much more likely to happen."

"Perhaps, but we're not going to risk a human life to find out," said Swayne.

Basil looked at him quizzically. "Funny how people shy away from the experimental method outside the laboratory. Perhaps because its answer is so final. That makes it a threat to any cherished theory. Don't you see that there is only one way to destroy the evil legend of this room now? Someone must spend the night there and wake in perfect health. And the sooner the better. You owe it to your daughter. Even if there were a real danger, I should feel it worth the effort because of Lucinda. As it is . . . Good God! Do you sit there, grown men, and tell me that you are afraid to sleep in

59

a room because it is haunted?"

Alcott laughed, but it was the cold laughter of indifference.

The others weren't laughing.

"You're right," said Swayne. "Dr. Willing, as far as I'm concerned, you may sleep in that room tonight and, as it's almost midnight now, you'd better get started."

"Wait a minute!" said Crowe. "It's still my house."

"But leased to me," retorted Swayne. "And there is no clause in that lease that says I cannot let anyone sleep in that room."

"You promised—"

"When I promised, I didn't foresee that my daughter's health might be involved. Neither did I foresee that I might be annoyed by a trickster faking poltergeist pranks. David, I want the key to that room now."

"You don't know what you're doing!" Crowe spoke to Swayne as if the others were not there. "I've lived with this story all my life. You haven't. Suppose something did happen tonight. You couldn't help feeling responsible. After all, three people have died in that room already for whatever reason. If there were a fourth death, there would be a dreadful feeling of inevitability about it."

"Nonsense," said Alcott. "Nothing is inevitable. Merely irrevocable."

"Isn't that the same thing?" said Crowe. "If the past determines the future, and the past is inalterable, then so is the future."

"And we're just threads in the dead hands of Clotho, Atropos and Lachesis?" Swayne was scornful. "Not even Flammarion's fragment of free will?"

Alcott smiled. "Oh, there's a fragment, but, as you get older, you have to watch it dwindle. At twenty your choices are almost unlimited. At fifty you're a prisoner of past decisions. At seventy you have no free will left at all. You have to surrender to the Three, whether you call them the Fates or the Norns or the Three Ladies of Britain."

Basil smiled. "If everything is inevitable, we can't make a decision. It's already been made for us."

There was an odd silence. Then Crowe spoke with resignation. "All right. I suppose everything has been leading up to this moment ever since I left the Thruway at Saugerties this evening, or perhaps ever since I was born. Here you are."

He fished in a hip pocket, took out a key and tossed it to Swayne, whose reflexes were in good working order, for he caught it in mid-air.

"Thanks." Swayne turned to Basil. "Aren't experiments supposed to be controlled? Perhaps if we have controls to eliminate certain possibilities, we can make David feel happier about the whole thing."

"What sort of controls?" Crowe's voice was loaded with suspicion.

"I don't think Willing or anyone else should volunteer to spend the night in that room. I think the four of us should draw lots."

"Why?"

"It's the fairest way to choose anybody if there's going to be any discomfort involved, and there will be discomfort because I'm going to suggest that whoever spends the night in that room shouldn't sleep at all. He should sit up all night. If anyone's playing tricks, or if there's anything wrong with the room physically, that's the only way to find out."

Alcott looked at Swayne thoughtfully. "Then you weren't entirely unimpressed by what I said?"

"On the contrary, I was so impressed that I'm going to suggest we keep my wife's parakeet, Tobermory, in the room all night. Birds are affected by bad air and poison gases more quickly than human beings. They've been used as air monitors in coal mines and trench warfare."

"Why don't we all spend the night in that room together?" said Crowe.

"I thought of that, but I don't believe it would work. Suppose someone is trying to make us believe this house is haunted. To make it convincing, a faker would follow tradition. According to tradition, raps come first, then an apparition. The raps may occur when there are several people present, but the apparition is more likely to be seen when someone is alone."

"For the obvious reason, I suppose?" put in Alcott.

"And that is?"

"That it's easier to fool one person than several people."

"Why would anyone want to fool you?" Basil asked Swayne. "To keep you from buying the house?"

"I suppose that's possible, if someone else is that anxious to buy the house."

"But damned improbable!" added Crowe.

"If it's just wanton mischief, whom would you suspect?" asked Basil.

"I've been thinking about that." Swayne sighed. "I would have said Vanya, but he telephoned just after we heard the raps. That lets him out. Are we all agreed now? Only one of us is to spend the night in that room, and he is to be chosen by lot?"

There was a murmur of assent. Out of it came Alcott's weary voice. "Suppose the poor devil falls asleep, bored to death all alone there?"

"He needn't be completely alone," said Swayne. "The rest of us can be within call here by the fire in the living room near the foot of the stairs with the hall door open. The haunted room is just at the head of the stair. If its door is left open, any sound up there could be heard down here. As for staying awake, he can have a thermos of strong, hot coffee and a good light and a book to read—preferably a controversial book that will keep his blood pressure up. And I think he should have a bell."

"Bell, book and candle!" cried Basil. "Why a bell?"

"Suppose he does . . . well . . . see something. He can ring the bell once. If something speaks to him, he can ring the bell twice. If something attacks him, he can ring the bell three times."

Basil grinned. "You're making my flesh creep with that 'something.' "

"What do you expect?" demanded Crowe. "The Nameless Horror from Outer Space?"

"Just getting into the spirit of the thing," returned Swayne. "I remember that bell business from an old folk tale of my childhood. It always did make my flesh creep. Imagine the feelings of the listeners hearing the bell ring twice and knowing that something was speaking at that very moment, yet not knowing what it was saying."

"Why the signals?" asked Crowe. "Ringing the bell once, twice and thrice. Why not just one ring three times?"

"One ring three times would simply indicate that something was happening. It wouldn't give you any idea what was happening. For that you need signals."

"And who would bother with all that?" Alcott was remotely amused. "If anybody attacked me, I'd just yell. When the others got upstairs, I could always tell them if I'd seen something and if it had spoken to me."

Crowe spoke quietly. "Providing you were still alive."

Basil turned to look at him incredulously. "I believe you really think that something is going to happen tonight."

Crowe answered in a voice tinged oddly with resignation. "I know that something is going to happen tonight."

7

THE KITCHEN WAS aggressively modern. Each decade has its fashion foibles. The signature of this one is the disintegration of the stove into its component parts. Basil was hardly surprised to see two ovens and a broiler in separate niches in three different walls while the surface of the stove was in a fourth corner between a dishwasher and a double sink. So far as he could discern, nothing was achieved except the multiplication of the number of steps the cook must take.

The woodwork and refrigerator which would have been white ten years ago were now jonquil yellow, and the linoleum and curtains which would have been yellow or some other cheerful color ten years ago were now an antiseptic white. At least the combination of yellow and white was still there to make the room seem sunny even at midnight.

Martha, the cook, had long gone to her own quarters in the garage and the four men had the place to themselves. Crowe was peering into an electric coffee percolator. "Already loaded for breakfast. All we have to do is plug it in."

Swayne was sitting on a high stool by one of the work counters. He had found a little memorandum pad bound in yellow leather, each page solemnly engraved with the word

Reminder—a reminder of a reminder. "Four slips of paper, each with a name . . ." He was thinking out loud. "One underlined."

"Why not four slips with a name on one?" suggested Alcott.

"This paper's thin. If only one slip were marked, we could all see which one it was from the other side."

"Afraid the man who draws will cheat?" Alcott was so haggard that his tired smile brought a flash of the death's-head grin beneath the flesh to the surface. "By avoiding his own name? Or by grabbing it?"

"If I were cheating, I'd grab," said Basil. "Curiosity."

"Coffee first." Crowe was taking cups and saucers down from a shelf, chaste white china with a thin rim of gold. "You know it's lucky we didn't have anything to drink after dinner. If we ever want to report this to some scientific journal, it will look awfully well if we can say we hadn't had a thing to drink since a hearty meal."

"I doubt if any scientific journal would be interested," said Basil. "And I for one have no intention of reporting this to any journal, scientific or otherwise. Probably ruin my reputation as a psychiatrist if it leaked out."

Alcott smiled again. "I see your point. Even if you reported that you'd only got involved in order to prove fraud, you'd still be in trouble with the extreme materialists for having got involved at all. Like saying: 'I am not and never have been a member of the Communist party.' "

Crowe poured coffee. Swayne took his cup and looked at the clock, a round, golden face without numerals, its brass hands shaped like two jet planes. No companionable ticking. In this kitchen it had to be electric, marking the flow of seconds with no sound to warn that your little lifetime was bleeding to death drop by drop.

"Ten after twelve," said Swayne.

Other glances were drawn to the clock. Deliberately they set down their cups. No one wanted to hurry.

Swayne himself took time to light a cigarette. At last he could think of no other excuse for postponing decision. He picked up the four slips of paper he had torn from the pad, then threw them down on the counter.

"Too flimsy. You can see through all of them. We need a pack of playing cards."

"I saw a pack in the living room," said Crowe. "I'll get it."

He was back in a minute. "New cards. Still in virgin cellophane." He broke the seal and began to shuffle them on the white porcelain top of the kitchen table. "Which is the fatal card?"

"Lowest card drawn," said Swayne. "And aces are high."

"Cut?" Crowe pushed the pack in front of Alcott.

"Thanks." Alcott cut the pack exactly in half and pushed it across the table to Basil. "We should all cut on a solemn occasion like this."

Basil's cut split the pack in one third and two thirds.

"I'll deal." Swayne scooped up the cards. Now there was silence as he put a card face down in front of each man at the table. "Well? Shall we turn them over?"

"Ace of hearts." Alcott sounded as indifferent to his fate as ever.

"Deuce of spades," said Crowe.

Basil looked at his own card. "King of diamonds."

Three pairs of eyes turned toward Swayne. He held up his card. It was the three of clubs. "You're it, David."

"I guess I am."

Crowe seemed aware of irony. He was the only one who had opposed unlocking the door to the haunted room, the only one who seemed to dislike the idea of the experiment. Basil had hoped to be chosen. Judging by externals, neither Alcott nor Swayne would have minded being chosen. But

Crowe did mind, and so . . . one of the Three Spinners had chosen Crowe. There was always a touch of malice in their fun.

"*Rien ne va plus!*" Crowe stood up. "I'm the only one related to Clotho, Atropos and Lachesis. Naturally they chose me."

Swayne was matter-of-fact. "We'll take the rest of the coffee upstairs and plug it in for you there."

"Oh, no, you won't. There's no place to plug it in. That room was locked up long before this house was wired for electricity."

"Oh? Then it'll have to be a thermos jug and you'll need a candle."

Swayne took a silver tray down from a high shelf, set it with napkin and spoon, cup and saucer, added cigarettes, matches, ash tray. He found a thermos jug on another shelf. There were candles in a drawer. "Anything else?"

"A book." Basil turned to Crowe. "What kind of book is most likely to keep you awake? Detective story?"

"Oh, no, I read those things to put me to sleep."

"What then?"

"Something controversial. One of those books that assumes the first steps from animal to human were intellectual and human rather than emotional and animal. I happen to believe that society invented man, not that man invented society."

"What about the granddaddy of them all, Freud's *Totem and Taboo?* It starts out with society already existing in the form of something called The Horde, whose origin is never explained. The transition from animal to human is attributed to ideas that are purely human—guilt, remorse and the concept of sexual taboos. That ought to keep anybody awake."

"Okay, I'll try it. You an anti-Freudian?"

"No." Swayne was leading the way back through the dining room, carrying the tray. "I just don't let myself forget that he was a Victorian whose first paper was published around 1895. His ideas, like Darwin's, need revising if they're to be kept up to date."

"What about the bell?" asked Crowe.

"Oh, yes." Swayne set down the tray and went back into the dining room. He returned in a moment with a bell of bright, hand-engraved brass dangling from a cord of twisted threads, red and white. He rang it experimentally. For so small a bell the sound was surprisingly deep, mellow and musical.

"Got it in Benares," he said. "It's not loud, but it's penetrating and quite loud enough. We'll hear it if you leave the door open."

"And if there's anything to hear," added Alcott.

"There probably won't be," Swayne was quick to agree. "A crowd of hard-headed skeptics with plenty of electric light will discourage most of these so-called manifestations whether they are illusion or fraud."

"But there won't be plenty of electric light," said Crowe quietly. "Remember?"

"Oh . . ." Swayne was at a loss for a moment. "But that's just in the one room. We'll leave electric light on in both halls, upstairs and down. And we'll have plenty of candles. How about this?"

"This" was a large, three-branched candlestick of curiously wrought iron standing on the great slab of rough-hewn stone that formed the chimney shelf. The candleholders were arranged in descending steps.

"Isn't all this pretty childish?" said Alcott suddenly. "I vote we all go to bed sensibly and forget the whole thing."

"I can't now," said Crowe.

"Why not?"

"I don't know . . . Momentum, Fate, something. I've got

to see it through now I've started it, even if all the rest of you go to bed . . . sensibly, as you put it."

"In that case the rest of us can hardly leave you in the lurch," said Swayne. "I'm like you. I'm too worked up to stop now. I must go on."

"But what is there to be worked up about?" Alcott's voice had never sounded more indolent. "Don't any of you have any idea how absurd this whole thing is going to seem by the light of day tomorrow morning?"

No one answered him.

"Well, if you won't give up, promise me this: that all four of us agree we'll never tell anyone else we were so silly."

"I'll agree to that," said Swayne. "And now let's get started. It's nearly half past twelve."

They mounted the stairs. Swayne took the key out of his pocket. The lock was rusty. It took a few moments' fiddling before the door swung open with a creak of its stiff, unoiled hinges.

The first thing that struck Basil about the room was that it was so small. To enter it, a tall man had to bend his neck as he passed under the lintel, and even a short man could touch the ceiling with his fingertips once he was in the room. Low ceilings always oppressed Basil. They suggested lairs and dens and fear, primitive humanity, cowering in dark, straitened places, hiding from great predators long ago.

The window revealed the thickness of the old stone walls in this part of the house. They were like short tunnels and there were only two of them, small casements with leaded panes. There wouldn't be much light here even by day.

The wide floorboards dipped toward one side of the room. Old foundations settled unevenly under the stress of freezing winters. Or was it so old that it was built before spirit levels were used? Walking on that sloping floor gave one a slight sensation of giddiness, like walking on the deck of a ship rolling in a stormy sea.

A gray bloom of lint furred everything. Dust had seeped through the cracks of locked doors and latched windows, settling evenly and smoothly for seventy years, mute witness to neglect.

"We should have brought a broom or a vacuum." Swayne's voice sank, a little abashed.

"Oh, let the dust be." Alcott spoke sardonically. "Let's see if this ghost can leave footprints."

Aside from the dust there was nothing that might not have been in any room in any fairly old house. A spoolbed, a Hitchcock rocking chair, a mahogany sewing table, a hooked rug, and, on the couch, a patchwork quilt worked in the log-cabin pattern. The very ordinariness of the room dispelled the vague fears they had all been ashamed to put into words.

"What a piece of Victoriana!" Alcott was looking at a round table, draped in olive green velvet, with a ball fringe that nearly touched the floor. It supported an oil lamp, Benares brass again, but much older than the bell. This had not been polished for generations. The lamp shade was white translucent china, molded in low relief, and hand-painted on the underside so that the colors would shine through dimly when it was lighted. There were four panels of hunting scenes, men and horses, foxes and hounds, men and deer, dogs and bears, all against backgrounds of evergreens and snow.

Swayne exclaimed suddenly. "We forgot Tobermory! I'll get him."

The others stood waiting a little awkwardly. The only light was coming from the hall. Crowe took some matches out of his pocket and lit the three candles in the wrought-iron candelabra. Their light pushed the darkness back a little way but the corners of the room were still shadowy.

"A pity you can't use that oil lamp," said Basil.

"Probably no wick after all these years," returned Crowe.

"And no kerosene in the house," added Alcott.

Swayne came back with the bird cage. Tobermory was wide awake, his head cocked to one side, his beady black eye moving restlessly. Swayne pushed the tray aside to make room for the bird cage on the table.

"It's rather cold in here," said Crowe.

"Yes." Swayne bent over a register grille in the floor. "This one is supposed to let heat through from the floor below, but it seems stuck. It won't open all the way."

"We could build you a fire." Basil was looking at the small stone fireplace in one corner.

"Oh, I'll be warm enough if you build up the fire downstairs," said Crowe. "This chimney is the same as the living-room chimney. Some of the heat is sure to come up. I suppose this rocking chair is the most comfortable seat. I'll move it nearer to the fireplace."

"You'll need a better light for reading." Swayne pushed the table with the candles on it nearer to the rocking chair. "And this bell should be hanging where you can reach it easily." He glanced at the wall, took down a small picture and hung the bell by its cord on the picture hook so that it dangled near Crowe's elbow.

"Okay?"

"Okay." Crowe sat down and leaned back, relaxing in the embrace of the rocking chair.

"Hey! Don't go to sleep on us!"

"More coffee? Or *Totem and Taboo?*"

"*Totem and Taboo,* I think." Crowe glanced at his wrist watch. "Almost one o'clock. Only a few more hours to cock-crow. Just about time to read *T. and T.*" He opened the book that lay on his knee.

Basil, nearest the door, was the first to move toward it. At the threshold he paused to look back.

Alcott stood in the middle of the room smiling at Crowe.

71

"Good luck!" He turned to follow Basil.

Swayne dropped a hand on Crowe's shoulder. "If you ring that bell, we'll be up in no time!"

Crowe didn't look up. He muttered something Basil was too far away to hear.

Down in the living room again, Basil studied Swayne's face. "Now you're worried."

"Silly, isn't it? But somehow leaving him there alone . . . Perhaps we shouldn't have let him do it."

"Why not?"

"He's lived with this odd story for a long time. He was brought up with it. It's part of his family history. I wish now that we'd stayed in the room with him. Or at least one of us."

"We can hardly change the thing now," said Basil.

"I know. He'd feel insulted. But I wish we hadn't done it this way and I wish we hadn't drawn lots. The victim should have been a volunteer."

Alcott, who had preceded them, was standing with his back to a roaring fire. He caught Swayne's last words.

"The victim is never a volunteer. In this life we're all conscripted sooner or later."

"I still don't like this. I wish I were up there instead of David."

"He'll survive. He'll laugh with the rest of us about all this in the morning."

"He didn't seem greatly worried when we left him," said Basil.

But Swayne shook his head. "He was putting it on. Bravado. I know him better than you do."

Basil tried to remember Crowe's tones, postures, gestures, but so tricky is memory that the immediate past is sometimes harder to recall than the remote past. Already the images of the last few hours had blurred and faded beyond the point where he could summon them to consciousness at will. Once

72

again he was reminded that the unconscious forces that govern accessible memory are the most arbitrary of editors and the absolute masters of our lives.

"Well, how are we going to keep awake?" demanded Alcott. "Cards?"

"Good idea." Swayne went into the kitchen and came back with the pack of cards they had left there. "Gin? Poker? Blackjack?"

"Poker ought to keep us awake."

They didn't bother with a card table. They pulled up three chairs to the coffee table in front of the fire.

"We need more light." Alcott moved the angel chimes to the middle of the table and lighted their four candles.

After the first round it was his turn to shuffle. Abruptly his hands were still. "Am I crazy? Or does that thing keep changing direction every now and then? I'm watching the angel on top. I swear he started clockwise, but now he's going widdershins like a witch casting a spell."

Basil smiled. "I've been all through this. We have one of those at home. The angels don't really change direction when they revolve, but if you watch the one on top, it looks as if they did. It's a peculiarly vivid optical delusion. Even now when I know they don't change direction, it still looks to me as if they did. It's like looking at a mirage. You tell yourself it isn't there, but there it is."

"Who knows what's there and what isn't?" said Swayne.

Alcott's eyes were still fixed on the top angel as if he were being hypnotized by the revolving motion. "There he goes again! I could swear he just changed direction."

"Let that be a lesson to you," retorted Swayne. "Showing how easily we can all be fooled by appearances. I wonder if David has gone to sleep. It's half an hour now since we left him up there and there hasn't been a sound."

Alcott was startled. "Good Lord! I'd forgotten him for a

few moments."

Swayne rose. "It's getting cold. I'd better put another log on."

Only a few charred embers were left of the fire that had been blazing so merrily half an hour ago, but there was still a glow of red under the film of gray ash. Swayne chose the thickest section of tree trunk in the wood basket. It slipped out of his grasp before he could place it properly on the dying embers and fell, raising a fountain of red sparks.

Alcott and Basil rose to stamp out those that reached the hearth rug. Swayne knelt with the bellows to coax the smoke and smolder into flame again. He must have chosen a well-seasoned log. With a muted roar a broad fan of yellow flame displaced the sluggish smoke and lighted up that whole end of the room.

Swayne rose, brushing his fingertips together. "You know, Brad, I really don't believe—"

The mellow note of a bell cut him off in mid-sentence. His eyeballs rolled toward the ceiling.

Alcott looked at Basil. "I don't believe it."

Basil had already reached the foot of the stairs, when the bell rang again, twice.

"But . . ." Alcott's voice faltered. "He was to ring twice if something spoke to him . . ."

Basil was on the stairs, Swayne close behind, Alcott following. As they reached the second landing, the bell rang three times.

At the top of the stairs a wedge of candlelight from the open doorway of the bedroom cut into the shadows of the upper hall. They paused in the doorway, one behind another, first Basil, then Swayne, then Alcott.

The room seemed as ordinary as it had before when they left it. Crowe still sat relaxed in the embrace of the rocking chair, his eyes cast down on the open book that lay upon his knee. There was no sign of another presence. The only marks in the dust on the floor were those from the doorway to the centre of the room and the rocking chair that they themselves had made half an hour ago.

Alcott was the first to speak. "I suppose you think this is funny? Seeing us all pelt up here to your rescue when it's nothing but a false alarm? Well, I don't. I've had enough. I'm going to bed now."

"Brad's right," said Swayne. "Let's just call the whole thing off."

"Did you hear what I said?" Alcott crossed the room to the rocking chair and put his hand on Crowe's shoulder.

"Wait." Basil followed swiftly. Crowe did not move or look up. Basil had to take the chin in one hand and lift it before he could look into the eyes.

He released the chin and turned to the others.

"It's too late to call it off. He's dead."

8

DAWN WAS NOT rosy-fingered that morning. Under heavy cloud all objects were bathed in a thin, equal light without spark, depth or shadow. It caught a full moon still high in the sky like an awkward guest who has outstayed his welcome. The whole scene was a painting by a primitive who could not lay his colors on canvas cunningly enough to invite reality.

Lucinda turned her eyes from the open window to the *chaise longue*. Folly was sleeping. The pillows behind her head were covered with the sheerest embroidered lawn over mauve-pink taffeta. Only her head and shoulders were visible above the hand-quilted coverlet of lilac satin. Her nightgown was frothy white, the neck threaded with mauve ribbon.

This nest of romantic color and Valentine lace softened the masculinity in her hard, handsome face. With eyes closed and lips parted in deep unconsciousness, she was at last disarmed if not innocent. Anyone else might have been touched by beauty so vulnerable, but her beauty only quickened Lucinda's hostility. It would have been easier to hate her if she had been old and ugly. Lucinda wanted to hate her.

Cautiously Lucinda laid back her bedcovers. Sudden movements made bed springs creak, so she moved with almost glacier-patience, sitting up and swinging her legs around until the soles of her bare feet met the cold floor silently. She waited. No sign from Folly.

Barefoot, Lucinda stepped softly to the door and opened it as slowly as she had disengaged herself from the bed. A moment later she was in the upper hall, closing the door behind her without a sound. Still Folly slept, but there were voices coming up the stairwell.

"Since the two men, Alcott and Swayne, were downstairs when Crowe rang the bell upstairs, they cannot possibly have killed him."

Lucinda's hand clenched the knob on the newel post at the head of the stairs. Killed him? Crowe? Who was this stranger who had just spoken in such an unfamiliar voice?

"Martha, the cook, sleeps over the garage, away from the house." That voice was Dr. Willing's. "I think you can safely eliminate her. We know that no one came to the house from outside because there were no marks in the snow which had just finished falling. That leaves four women and a girl who were upstairs on the same floor with Crowe when he died: Crowe's own wife, Serena; Alcott's wife, Ginevra; Swayne's wife, Eleanor Folsom Swayne who's known as Folly. And, of course, Swayne's daughter. Lucinda, isn't it?"

How odd to hear your own name spoken so coldly and yet so casually and familiarly by a man you have never met.

"Yes. She's only fifteen. She was in a highly emotional state last night and we put her to bed with a sedative. We didn't wake her afterward."

"Four women altogether. No, five. You forgot your own wife, Dr. Willing."

"A Freudian error, Captain Marriott. Even my unconscious mind knows that she is not involved."

Captain Marriott? State Police from the barracks at Leeds?

"Technically all these ladies had a physical opportunity to

kill Crowe."

"Yes," answered Basil. "But so far as I can see now, not one of them had a motive."

There was a creaking sound as if someone heavy had shifted position in a light chair.

"Are you telling me that the men couldn't have killed Crowe and the women wouldn't?"

Basil countered with another question. "Have you eliminated all possibility of natural death?"

"I can't until I get the autopsy report, but I already have a feeling that there is more to it than that."

"Why? Consider the facts as we know them. My wife and I arrived here only a few hours ago and we had never met any of these people before. The two other men were downstairs with me when Crowe died. The four women and the young girl who went upstairs are the sort who would murder only under extreme stress. Only one of them showed any sign of stress at all last night, the girl, Lucinda, when she—"

Gee, thanks a lot! Lucinda scowled in the direction of the stairwell. She thought of sticking out her tongue, but that would be childish. She thought of swearing under her breath, but owing to the ludicrously old-fashioned atmosphere at home and at school her vocabulary was limited. The only words she could think of were hell, damn, bastard and bitch, and that wasn't swearing. That was the way everybody talked all the time in books. She wasn't reading the right books. She must ask Vanya to give her a list of the others. . . .

". . . so you see no connection between her fainting fit and Crowe's death?"

"Not at the moment." Basil's answer came slowly, as if he were not quite sure of this opinion. "I must concede that when two inexplicable things happened at about the same time and place, there is likely to be some connection between them, but I can't see one here. Not yet."

78

"You have no idea why she fainted?"

"No, you'll have to ask her when she wakes."

"Could it be she was just scared by those rapping noises?"

"She didn't look scared up to the moment she fainted. On the contrary, she seemed to be rather enjoying the excitement. If I thought the rappings were a practical joke, she'd be the first I'd suspect."

Bastard . . .

"She didn't faint until she got that telephone call."

"But you don't think the faint was a fake?"

"No, that was real. I know, because I examined her. By that time something had frightened her very much indeed."

"And you have no idea what caused the rapping noises?"

There was a pause before the answer came. A pause for consideration. Or just a pause to put out a cigarette? Lucinda had no way of knowing. This was like listening to television when the picture tube is dead.

"I can't answer that. I'd just be guessing."

"And you really think Crowe may have died from natural causes?"

"Again that's just a guess. There was nothing about his body that suggested any other cause to a casual observer—no external wounds, no signs of poisoning or suffocation. Only a post-mortem can answer the question properly. I'd suggest a thorough one."

"It'll be thorough. There's one question we must answer somehow. Why did he ring that bell three times before he died? He was supposed to ring it only if he was attacked. That bothers me."

"It bothers me, too. I dare say Crowe took the ghost story more seriously than he admitted. Most people are ashamed to admit taking such things seriously, but things you learn when you're very young make as deep an impression on human beings as on animals. It's what zoologists call 'imprinting.'

79

Crowe had grown up with that story. When we left him alone in that so-called haunted room, he may have been wound up to a pretty high pitch. Pulse, respiration, blood pressure—the works."

Haunted room? Lucinda's eyes fled to the closed door at the head of the stairs. Had Crowe died in there? Alone? What was he doing in there?

"After he'd sat there alone for nearly an hour, he'd be wound up even tighter. If he heard, or thought he heard, some sound . . . If his candle-flame flickered and a shadow moved and he thought he saw more than a shadow moving . . . He'd be likely to ring that bell, especially if he were a little too breathless to cry out. And such panic might be just too much for his heart if there was any cardiac weakness at all."

"Were there just three rings? Or was the bell rung several times each time it rang, with a total of three times?"

"There were three times when it rang. They were distinct, but quite close together. The sound was too blurred to count the rings distinctly each time."

"So we don't really know whether he was trying to follow the signal system or not?"

"You mean one ring for anything he saw, two for anything that spoke to him, and three for anything that attacked him? No, it would be impossible to say whether he was trying to follow that signal system or not."

"Any record of cardiac weakness in his medical history?"

"You'll have to ask his doctor, but people can die of heart failure without any record of previous trouble."

The sound of a yawn. Lucinda was shocked. Did policemen finally become so used to crime that they could feel sleepy in the middle of an investigation? Even if they'd been up half the night, they had no right to yawn.

"How about more coffee? Martha has just brought some

into the dining room. Hot and fresh."

Lucinda was surprised to hear her father's voice. Why hadn't he spoken before? Then she realized that Dr. Willing's work with the district attorney's office in New York would give him a privileged status anywhere in New York state, while her father was merely a witness or perhaps even a suspect in the eyes of the police. He had probably just come into the room from the dining room as the discussion ended.

"Hot coffee sounds great."

Footfalls receded. Silence flowed into the rooms below, like a quietly rising tide.

She was sure there was no one there now, but she had the habit of stealth. She tiptoed to the door of the room at the head of the stairs and turned the knob. Locked. What could have happened in there last night?

On the stairs she trod softly. In the lower hall was a closet under the stairs for outdoor wraps. She found her ski boots, parka and mittens there. Her wool slacks were in her own room upstairs where Mrs. Willing was sleeping, but her flannel pajamas were thick and warm and the parka was a little big for her so it came down well below her hips. She wouldn't be cold. She zipped up the parka, drew the hood over her head and tied the drawing strings under her chin.

The living room was cold. She glanced at the hearth. There was a roseate glow at the core of white ashes, yet no one had bothered to put up the fire screen. That showed how upset they must be. Fear of fire is engrained in all who live in lonely woods that can turn to tinder during drought, especially when the house is far from urban water supplies. Automatically she took the poker to break up the embers and extinguish them before putting up the fire screen.

Yes, under the flaky white ash there was a fairly large chunk of red-hot coal. She paused. Something in the ashes caught her eye.

The poker was one of those with a point bent at a right angle to the rest of the shaft. That made it easy to hook the tiny object and draw it toward her. She knelt to look at it more closely.

A thin, flexible strip of metal, bent slightly in the centre at a wide angle. There was a small hole near the centre that looked as if it might have held a screw there once. Now what could that be?

She dropped it in the pocket of her parka and went on breaking up the embers. For a moment she looked longingly at the telephone, but no. She didn't dare. Someone here might overhear what she said. Or Vanya's mother might answer the call at the other end. Besides, she mustn't stay in the living room too long. Dr. Willing or her father or the police might come back at any moment and then she would have no freedom of movement.

At the very thought her heart missed a beat, but, even then, she took time to put up the fire screen in front of the fire before she went to the front door.

The outdoor air was cold, pure and sweet. Plunging into it was like diving into a mountain lake. She paused at the head of the steps. Footprints in the snow between the house and an empty car in the driveway with the arms of New York state on its door. Tire tracks in the driveway. Footprints on the path to Martha's quarters in the garage. Everywhere else the snow was a blank page.

She went down the steps, carefully fitting her feet into the larger footprints already there. Under the steps was a door to a closet for skis and poles. She took out her own skis and sat down on the bottom step to put them on. She thrust her icy hands into fleece-lined, fur mittens and began to glide down the driveway around its steep and sudden curves. She was leaving a clear trail, but that couldn't be helped here. Once she got as far as the road, any trail she left would be soon obliterated by tire tracks.

Between the trunks of two tall pines she saw evidence that someone else had been abroad early—a fox—but still there was no sign of human tracks anywhere near the house save those she was making now.

On the road the slope leveled out and her progress was slower, but that didn't worry her. She was beyond sight of the house now. There was no reason to hurry unless she heard a hue and cry behind her, and then she could discard her skis and take to the deep woods where underbrush would make it hard to follow her quickly. If only it were summer! Then a few yards into the woods and she would be completely hidden. But in winter, with leafless trees and half the underbrush dead, it was harder to hide.

She went nearly a mile before she came to a fork in the road and swerved left. Now she could see the chimneys of Vanya's house among the tops of pine trees. The house stood in a hollow, below the level of the road. She took off her skis and carried them the rest of the way. If anyone did try to track her from the ski marks she had left in her own driveway, they would be looking for more ski tracks here, not for footprints. She kicked her feet as she set them down so the tracks would be blurred and enlarged. She hoped the added weight of the skis would make it look as if a heavier person had walked here.

She came to a halt at the back of the house under the windows of Vanya's room. Beside the kitchen door were rosebushes in winter overcoats of straw. She groped under the snow until she found a few of the pebbles that lay around the roots of the roses in summer.

When the fifth pebble struck the windowpane, the window opened and Vanya leaned out, hair tousled, eyelids heavy with sleep.

"Oh, it's you, Worm. What the hell—?"

"Sh-sh. Not so loud, Vanya. I must talk to you at once."

"What time is it?"

"About six o'clock."

"God, are you nuts? I'm going back to sleep."

"No, Vanya! Things have happened. Lots of things. Can't you come dowstairs and let me into the kitchen? If you're careful, your mother won't wake up."

"What happened?"

"I can't tell you standing here. If we go on talking as loud as this, your mother will wake up. Be a sport! Let me in. You'll be sorry, if you don't."

"Okay, okay. I'll come down."

He closed the window without making a sound.

She hadn't noticed the cold while she was skiing, but now, standing still, she felt cold. She propped the skis against the wall of the house and hunched her shoulders, crossing her arms over her chest, trying to hold the warmth of her body in, but it didn't do any good. She was shivering. Would he go back to sleep after all and just leave her standing there?

The door opened and she saw the reason for the delay. He had stopped to put on loafers and slacks and sweater.

"You needn't have dressed." She brushed past him. "Every moment counts."

"You're scared." He eyed her speculatively. "What's up?"

"All sorts of things and I am scared. I'm not going to pretend I'm not. David Crowe died last night. The State Police are at the house now. I slipped out when they were in the dining room. No one knows I'm here. They think I'm still asleep."

"David Crowe's dead? How did he die?"

"I don't know how he died. I don't know anything about it. I was asleep when it happened. But I did overhear the police talking to Dr. Willing just now. They said something about that room at the head of the stairs. The one that's always locked. The one that's supposed to be haunted. I think he died in there and—" Her voice winced, but she forced it on. "I think he was murdered."

"Nothing to do with you or me," said Vanya quickly.

"Oh, yeah?"

"Pull yourself together, Worm, and I'll make you some coffee."

"Do you know how?"

"It's instant."

"Ugh! How icky!"

"You're lucky to get that." He plumped a mug down in front of her, but in a spoonful of powdered coffee and two spoonfuls of sugar.

"I want a saucer. I'm civilized."

"So am I, but my mother isn't." His voice went higher, a parody of affectation. *"Won't you have some coffee, my deah? In a mug, of course. We are mug people."*

"Well, I'm not a mug person. I want a saucer and a spoon."

"Okay." He pushed a butter plate under the mug and handed her a battered kitchen spoon. The kettle began to whistle. He poured hot water into her cup.

"Why is your mother like that?"

"Like what?"

"Mug people."

"Oh, it's the time when she was growing up, I guess. The thirties. There was a lot of inverted snobbery around then. A lot of people were broke and made a virtue of necessity. Cheap crockery instead of china, wooden beads instead of pearls, a poster from some travel agency instead of a good engraving. It was all of a piece and they never got over it. My mother's still talking the way people did then. Do you know she still reads Pavlov and all his camp followers and takes them seriously? She tells everyone that I'm an outgoing boy and well adjusted to the group because she never spoiled me. Of course the whiz now is not to adjust to the group, and God knows I work at it, but she doesn't even realize that conformism is old-hat. People don't outlive their youth. Everybody dies at thirty."

"Do you suppose we will? Will we have children someday who'll think we're old-hat?"

"No. We'll be different." He sang softly:

"The sun may rise and shine at night,
Birds swim and fish take flight . . ."

Lucinda joined in the chorus:

"Heigh-ho, it's still all right,
We'll be the same . . . Only we won't, of course."

"No, we won't." Vanya sat down beside her, warming his hands around his own mug of coffee. "It's easy to laugh at old age when you haven't seen twenty yet . . ." She put up her mouth and he kissed her. "Aren't you afraid you'll pick up my virus?"

"I'm not scared of viruses."

"What are you scared of?"

"Vanya . . . were you really here last night at nine o'clock when you telephoned me? I want the truth! Don't you dare snow me! If you do, I'll never forgive you."

Something in her voice sobered Vanya. "I was here, Worm. Awful sore throat I had. Of course I wanted to go out. I wanted to go over to your house and carry out our plan. I even told my mother you were expecting me, when all else failed. But she wouldn't listen. She made me take aspirin and hot lemonade and go to bed. So I called you before I went to bed and I must have been asleep a few minues later. Calling you is about the last thing I remember clearly. If you don't believe me, ask my mother. But . . . why are you asking me?"

"It happened."

"What did?"

"The raps. And you weren't there."

Vanya set down his mug. "Are you kidding?"

"No. It was just before you telephoned. So, when it happened, I thought of course that it was you making the raps."

"Well, I'll be . . . Of course old houses do creak a bit at night, but—"

"No, Vanya, it wasn't that."

"How do you know?"

"Don't you understand? I really did think it was you making the noises. After all, we had planned everything so carefully. Remember?"

"Of course."

"I carried out our plan. I—" Her mouth trembled. "I shouted: *Do as I do, Mr. Splitfoot!* And I clapped my hands three times, and . . ."

"And what?"

Her eyes filled. "Oh, Vanya, there were three raps in response."

It was her first experience of the fact that even we ourselves do not always realize how deeply we are being moved until we reach the peak of a crisis. All morning she had been as tightly wound as a coiled spring. She had felt as if she would never relax again. Now, putting her fear into words brought on the shock of total realization. Under that shock everything was breaking.

Tears slid down her cheeks, but her eyes were wide open and she didn't sob. It was the first time she had ever wept without crying, the first time she had ever experienced the personality split which reduces tears to a purely physical reaction.

The water in her eyes was a prism refracting light in various colors. Through the dazzle, she could see Vanya's stunned face.

"You swear it wasn't you?"

"It wasn't. I swear."

She saw fear in his eyes as great as her own. After that, she couldn't doubt him.

"Then . . . if it wasn't you . . . what was it? Oh, God, what was it?"

9

GISELA HEARD voices before she opened her eyes—a distant murmur. There was a pause, then the murmur again. She opened her eyes.

She was lying on her side and the first thing that met her gaze was an unfamiliar wall papered in cream-color with a design of moss rosebuds in pale green and pink. She twisted over on her back. Sharp pain stabbed one ankle and she felt a bandage. Full consciousness came back in a flood. Snow . . . Crow's Flight . . . Dinner . . . *Do as I do, Mr. Splitfoot!* Voices . . . Noises in the night . . . Basil and men in uniform. *Sorry to trouble you, Mrs. Willing, but there has been a sudden death—Mr. Crowe. He died in the room at the head of the stairs. It looks like a death from natural causes, but we would like to know if you heard anything during the night? . . . Nothing at all? . . . Thank you so much . . .*

A tap on the door. Police again?

Gisela reached for the fluffy pink mohair dressing gown beside the bed and called: "Come in!"

To her relief it was Basil, bearing coffee.

"Oh, thank you, darling. Is it terribly late?"

"Terribly. Twelve noon. But there was no particular

89

reason for wakening you before."

"What happened last night? I was only half awake when the police asked me if I'd heard anything. I hardly remember what they said. Do tell me about it."

She sipped her coffee as she listened, her eyes growing rounder. At last she set down the empty cup.

"I feel as if we had skied right off the map last night into one of those vast, empty spaces marked on old charts: *Here Be Dragons.*"

"So do I. All that bell, book and candle business seems so silly now. Of course none of us expected to trap a ghost. I wanted to prove to Swayne that there was nothing to trap. I think the others were hoping we might unmask the joker who made those rapping noises. If there was a joker to unmask, opening up the haunted room would give him—or her—an opportunity hard to resist."

"And it was just coincidence that David Crowe happened to die in the middle of all this?"

"Was it?" Basil sighed. "Then . . . why did he ring that bell? Surely if he'd felt the sudden chest pains of a heart attack, he'd have called out to us, wouldn't he?"

"You say that each time the bell rang the rings were all run together and blurred so you couldn't tell if he was ringing once or twice or thrice. Wouldn't the rings blur if he was in pain or frightened?"

"But why ring at all? That's what bothers me. If something really frightened him, wouldn't he have forgotten all about bells and signals and shouted for us? Real fear produces real response. If you think you're going to die, you run or yell or fight. You don't just sit there, tinkling a little bell because you said you would if anything happened to you."

"But that's what Crowe did, so that proves . . . what?"

"It doesn't prove anything, but it suggests a lot. Perhaps he wasn't really frightened when he rang the bell. Perhaps he

90

didn't expect to die."

"You mean that Crowe himself was playing some kind of trick or joke on the rest of you and it went wrong?"

"That's one possibility."

"But . . . if he was . . ." Gisela hesitated.

"You don't like to say it, do you?"

"Say what?"

"What you are obviously going to say: If he was playing a trick or joke on us, wouldn't he need a confederate? And wouldn't the confederate, who knew all about the trick, be the person most likely to kill him, using the trick to distract our attention from the real situation, murder?"

"Another man? I can see two men planning a trick like that together, but somehow not a man and a woman."

"Yet in these circumstances, the confederate is more likely to have been a woman."

"Why?"

"All the men have alibis. Alcott, Swayne and I were all together downstairs after we left Crowe alone in the room upstairs and we stayed together until the bell rang and Crowe was found dead. No one could have got to Crowe from outside the house. There were no tracks or footprints in the new-fallen snow around the house when the police arrived last night. No man could have got to Crowe inside the house. All the time Crowe was upstairs, Alcott, Swayne and I were sitting in the living room near the open door into the lower hall where we could see the stairs. We didn't watch it every moment, but I do not believe anyone could have gone up that stairway without our seeing or hearing him. And there is no other stair. So it would seem as if the only people who do not have alibis are the women who were in the bedrooms upstairs."

"If one of the women had gone along the hall to the haunted room, would you have heard her?"

"I don't know. There is one floorboard that creaks up there. I noticed it yesterday. On the other hand we might not have heard a single creak. We were all talking and playing cards. . . . We didn't think Crowe was in any real danger. We assumed that if anything frightened him, he'd ring the bell. . . . Oh, well, it's not my case, thank God! How's the ankle this morning?"

"Let's see." Gisela swung her legs to the floor and tried to rise, clinging to the bedpost.

"Can you walk?" He gave her his arm.

She took a few steps, leaning on him heavily.

"Worse?"

"I'm afraid so. I can't even stand without pain this morning, let alone walk."

"Sounds like a fracture. We'll have to get you to a hospital and have some X-rays this morning."

"And that means a cast?"

"A walking cast in a day or so, and crutches. But not for very long. Stay here in bed and I'll see what arrangements I can make."

Captain Marriott was standing in front of the hearth in the living room watching as a young trooper used the fire shovel to remove ashes from the fireplace and deposit them on a newspaper. He was young for a captain, or perhaps he merely seemed younger than he was because his eyes were such an innocent shade of blue and so intensely serious.

When he saw Basil, he seemed to think some explanation was necessary. "Thought we might as well look through this stuff in the grate. If there's a fire handy, people will throw small things in to get rid of them."

"So I see." Basil looked with distaste at three cigarette stubs, an empty cigarette pack, rather crumpled, a scrap of paper envelope scorched around the edges, two tenpenny nails and, worst of all, the core of an apple beginning to turn brown.

Captain Marriott noticed his look. "I feel the way you do. It's no way to treat an indoor hearth, but a lot of people don't realize that. They seem to think an ordinary fire will consume anything. Even professional criminals make that mistake sometimes, and when they do, it can be a big help to us."

Basil looked at him quickly. "You're thinking in terms of crime?"

"I have to until the autopsy report comes through. . . . Now what would that be?"

It was a tiny object, so tiny that only its creamy white color made it stand out among the gray-white ashes. Marriott picked it up and showed it to Basil lying on the palm of his hand. A little elephant, carved in hard-looking, white material. Too hard to be plastic. Ivory? You didn't carve plastic, you molded it, and this delicate definition of fine detail suggested hand carving. If it was ivory, it must be old, for it was the dingy yellowish white of old lace.

"I suppose it might be Japanese," said Basil. "They carve tiny objects in ivory called *netsuké*."

He turned it over with one finger. On the other side, now revealed, there was a dot—a minute perforation with a faint ring of rust around its edge. "At some time this little elephant has been attached to something metallic. It looks as if it might have been an old-fashioned hatpin made from a *netsuké*."

"I wonder what it's doing here? And I wonder what happened to the rest of it?" Marriott laid it down carefully in a clean ash tray on the table beside him. "You have something on your mind?"

Basil told him about Gisela.

93

"She may have to spend a night or so in the hospital. Once she's comfortable, I'll probably go on to the ski lodge where we have rooms reserved, unless you need me for something here."

"Well . . ." Marriott smiled suddenly and disarmingly. "At the moment I feel as if I needed all the help I could get. I've been talking to the district attorney in New York about you. Called him early this morning. From what he said, I gather you've had offbeat cases like this before. What's more, you were on the spot here when it happened. Perhaps you'd stop by on your way to the ski lodge after leaving Mrs. Willing at the hopsital. We may have a preliminary autopsy report by that time."

"I'll be glad to do that."

"Oh, you will, will you?"

The mocking, cackling voice startled all three men.

"Who said that?" demanded Marriott, looking toward the dining room.

"Came from outside, I think, sir." The young trooper started toward the front door.

"You're both wrong," said Basil. "Look at the centre table."

They turned and looked and stood speechless.

The high, brass bird cage stood in the middle of the table. Tobermory was sidling along his perch, preening feathers of jade and turquoise brilliant as tropical seas. Beady eyes were fixed on Basil. The cackle came again.

"Three cheeahs for good old Hahvahd!" A gasp, a gurgle. Was that meant for a laugh? "Not loud enough to be vulgah . . . But loud enough to be heahd. . . . Splitfoot . . . Splitfoot . . . Splitfoot . . . toobroo . . . toobroo . . . toobroo . . ."

Basil studied the bird with fascination. "To think he was there in that room last night when Crowe died. He saw and

94

heard everything that happened. If only he could really talk . . ."

"But he can't," said Marriott. "Those birds are just echoes. They don't know what they're saying. They're like tapes. They record without understanding."

"But they do record," said Basil thoughtfully.

Tobermory cackled again. "Shall I freshen up your drink? . . . Why don't you bring your drinks to the table? . . . Toobroo . . . toobroo . . . toobroo . . ."

"What's that he's saying now?" asked Marriott.

"To me it sounds like *to brood,*" said Basil.

"And to me it sounds like gibberish." Swayne had just come into the room from the dining room. He spoke lightly, but his eyes were troubled.

10

VANYA WAS BEING masterful. "What you need is more coffee, Worm," he told Lucinda. "You're getting hysterical."

"I'm not hysterical. Just scared." She shivered and her thin hands clasped the mug of hot coffee as if she were trying to warm them. "Aren't you?"

Vanya paused, turning the question around in his mind, examining it from every point of view. "Yes, I am rather," he admitted. "But I'm more fascinated than scared. Aren't you?"

Lucinda smiled one of her pale smiles. "When I'm with you and it's daylight—yes. But when I'm alone and it's dark . . . Vanya, don't you think it's time you told me where you were going to hide if you had made those raps?"

"No, I don't. A secret shared is a secret lost."

"Well . . ." Lucinda smiled again. "You don't have to tell me now. I know."

"What!"

"I found out by accident yesterday afternoon. I was trying to slide down that ramp thing in the upper hall and the wall gave way under my hand. Oh, Vanya, it's the most wonderful secret in the world! You were mean not to tell me before.

After all, it's my house, not yours."

"Well I'll be damned . . ."

"That is where you were going to hide, isn't it?"

"Of course. That's what gave me the whole idea of the poltergeist caper in the first place. It's such a perfect hiding place."

"And such a perfect listening post. You can hear everything that's said in the bedrooms and the living room."

"You can? Are you quite sure?"

"Of course I'm sure. Didn't you know?"

"I explored the house when it was empty before you moved in. There was nothing to overhear."

"Well, you can. I heard the Crowes talking yesterday in their bedroom when they first got there. They were quarreling."

"What about?"

"He was saying she was . . . well, paying too much attention to some other man, and she kept saying she wasn't. It was just like listening to television when you can't see the screen."

"Who was the other man?"

"He didn't say."

"You're sure it was the Crowes you heard?"

"Oh, yes. I know their voices. Besides, he called her Serena."

"I wonder if this could have anything to do with the murder?"

"Motive? Lover kills husband because lover wants to marry wife?"

"Or wife kills husband because she wants to marry lover."
Vanya scraped at a spot on the linoleum with the toe of his loafer. "There must be some reasonable explanation for the murder. And there must be some reason for the poltergeist bit, too. You realize that, don't you?"

"No, I don't," said Lucinda. "And you didn't talk as if you thought there was a reasonable explanation for poltergeists yesterday."

"That was yesterday." He grinned. "Your eyes do get so round when I tell you that sort of thing. You show a rim of white all around the iris, like a frightened horse. The temptation is irresistible."

"What temptation?"

"*Epater le* . . . What's the French for Worm? *Ver?*"

"Stop calling me Worm in any language and tell me what you mean."

"I enjoy scaring you. Or rather I did enjoy scaring you yesterday, but now I'm beginning to get scared myself. I can't believe a knocking spirit answered you when I wasn't there to fake it, but what did happen? Why would anyone else fake it, and how? Then there's another thing. You and I know a lot of things the police don't know, things that a murderer might not want the police to know, like Crowe's being jealous of his wife. I wonder if that's healthy . . . for us . . ."

"We don't know anything really significant."

"Are you sure? We know about the attic, and we know that we planned that poltergeist trick."

"Are those things significant?"

"They may be. We just don't know."

"I suppose you're going to say we ought to tell the police all that now?"

Vanya threw her a dark, reproachful look. "Really, Worm! You should know me better than that."

"I said stop calling me Worm."

He went on as if she hadn't spoken. "You don't know me very well, or you wouldn't even suggest I'd say anything like that. No, I was going to say that—with all we know that the police don't know—you and I should be able to solve this case and find the murderer long before they do."

"Oh, Vanya!" Lucinda looked at him with a respect that must have satisfied even his adolescent ego. "You are wonderful! How do we go about it? Will we have to draw up lists of suspects and timetables and all that sort of thing?"

"Certainly not!" said Vanya. "That's the part I always skip in detective stories. The really good ones don't even put it in."

"Then what do we have to do?"

"Think."

"That's harder than drawing up lists and timetables."

"I know, but, unfortunately, it's necessary."

Lucinda waited a minute or so while he thought with ostentatiously knitted brows. At last she ventured an interruption. "Vanya, what are we supposed to be thinking about?"

"The murder, of course."

"But what part of the murder?"

"Well, for one thing, is there any way the murderer could have found out about our poltergeist plan? Could he have used it as part of his murder plan? Could it have been he who made the answering raps when you called out: *Do as I do, Mr. Splitfoot?*"

"Why would a murderer do that?"

"I don't know why, but . . . could he have faked it? Could anyone have faked it? You were there. I wasn't. You tell me."

"I don't see how anyone could. Everybody in the house was in the living room with me when it happened except Martha, the cook, and it couldn't have been Martha."

"Why not?"

"She's too dignified. Besides, she was in the kitchen and that's on the other side of the dining room, much too far from the living room. The people who were in the living room were all in full view of one another and no one was moving when the answering knocks came. After it was over, everybody was too shocked and surprised to move for a few moments. And then the telephone rang. That was your call."

"You can fake looking surprised, of course," said Vanya. "It would be harder to fake not moving while you were making the raps. I don't see how anyone could."

"Neither do I."

"What direction did the raps come from?"

"Oh, Vanya, how can I tell? You know how hard it is to tell where a sound comes from if you have no visual clue. That's been proved by experiment in psychological laboratories."

"I know, I know, but still . . . Haven't you any idea at all?"

"No, I haven't. Oh, how I wish the thing had worked out the way we planned it in the first place! The raps would have sounded so scary coming from the other side of the wall. Just think how scared They would have been if They had looked for a way to get to the other side of the wall and hadn't been able to find any!"

"I know. It was a perfect set up and then I had to go and get a sore throat and spoil everything!"

"I wonder what would have happened if you hadn't got a sore throat?"

"That's a thought. I would have been scared witless hiding alone in the dark attic if answering knocks had come before I had time to fake them. Gosh!"

"And I would have thought it was you faking them all the time when it wasn't."

Vanya shook his head dubiously. "If the faker wasn't someone in the living room, he must've been someone outside the house."

"With all that snow and no footprints anywhere near the house?"

"None at all?"

"When the raps started, Daddy opened the front door to see if anyone was knocking. There wasn't anybody, of course. The snow was still falling and there weren't any prints."

"You mean there weren't any in front of the house. How about the back and sides."

"Wouldn't the police look when they came in the middle of the night after Crowe died? Wouldn't they be looking now for someone outside the house if they'd found any prints then?"

"So it all comes down to this: the raps couldn't have been made by anyone inside the house or by anyone outside the house."

"I know." Lucinda's voice faltered. "Vanya, do you think perhaps there really is a Mr. Splitfoot?"

"No, I don't."

"Not a devil or a poltergeist or a ghost but . . . well . . . forces . . ."

"Nonsense! There has to be some rational explanation and it's up to us to find it. Did Mrs. Crowe show any signs of interest in any particular man last night?"

Lucinda shook her head.

"Were you watching her?"

"Naturally after what I'd heard. She talked to all the men. She didn't concentrate on any particular one."

"She wouldn't, of course." Vanya was sadly cynical. "They don't. They hide these things from their husbands."

"Well, you'd hardly expect her to tell him, would you? Unless she wanted a divorce? Still it is kind of odd. I wouldn't have thought she was that sort of woman."

"Why not? People who run off the rails look and talk just like everybody else."

"I suppose so, but—"

"But what? She seems so good and noble?"

"No, she's not a bit like that. I don't like her, really. She smarms all over me, but I know she doesn't mean a word of it. She's just making up to Folly and Daddy through me, because Daddy is one of her husband's most profitable authors."

"Well, then, she sounds just like the sort of phony who would—"

"No, Vanya, she isn't." Lucinda struggled for words to express an idea beyond her own experience. "Don't you see that if a person got involved in a tragedy like murder through—well—passion—there would have to be a certain greatness about the passion? At least it would have to be overwhelming. But I don't believe Serena Crowe is capable of feeling or inspiring anything great. She's shallow, self-centred, trivial."

"And you're a baby or you've read the wrong books," said Vanya. "You probably get your ideas from *Anna Karenina* and *Madame Bovary*. People don't have grand passions like that any more. They just have sex, and sex can be just as trivial and self-centred as anything else in life."

"All right, but those people don't commit crimes of passion. If your feeling for somebody is trivial and self-centred, you're not going to risk your life for that somebody and he's not going to risk his life for you."

"Oh, I don't know." Vanya was a little beyond his depth, but still swimming valiantly. "It could be like getting drunk, you know. Running *amok*. Going *berserk*. Something people do for excitement, not love."

Lucinda laughed. "It's easy to see the kind of books you've been reading. The kind reviewers call 'frank,' 'fearless,' 'earthy' and 'adult.' In real life people are moved by love and fear and interest, but not by sex. It's just something they like to read about."

"Maybe she was after money rather than love," suggested Vanya.

"Bradford Alcott is the only man here you could call rich," said Lucinda. "And he's so old he's practically dead. I can't see any man being jealous of a corpse, can you?"

"There's your father—"

"Leave him out of it!"

"Well, then, there isn't anybody. Dr. Willing wasn't here when you overheard the Crowes talking."

"Oh, yes, he was. The Willings arrived just before the Crowes, but from the way they talked at dinner, I don't think the Willings had met anyone here before last night."

"So that lets Dr. Willing out and we're right back where we started. We have no idea who Mrs. Crowe's lover was. Did they speak as if he were there in the house last night?"

"Crowe did. Very plainly."

"And you're sure it was the Crowes?"

"I've known them for years. I'd know their voices anywhere. Hers is flat and nasal. His is rather high-pitched for a man, but wiry and vibrant, especially when he's upset, and he was upset last night. He was really jealous."

"And he was the one who got killed. That gives us such a beautiful motive for the lover . . . if only we knew who the lover was."

"I still can't imagine any man risking his life for a woman like Serena Crowe."

"That's what people always say about these crimes of passion," retorted Vanya. "Just look up the records, especially the photographs of the women, and you won't be able to believe that such commonplace faces could drive some poor devil to crime."

"Commonplace is the word for Serena Crowe."

"Then she's just the sort of woman a man would commit

murder for, only . . ."

"Only what?"

"When a man kills for a woman it's usually because he can't get her any other way, because she's too respectable or religious or something to divorce her husband. Is Serena like that?"

"No. The kind of people she knows wouldn't care whether she was divorced or not, and I know she's not religious."

"Then why murder?"

"Could it be that this lover was afraid Crowe would kill him? Self-defense?"

"I don't believe a planned murder would be called self-defense."

"We don't know that the murderer did any planning," objected Lucinda. "You and I planned the poltergeist bit."

"You think the murderer acted on the spur of the moment, taking advantage of plans made by other people?"

"Why not? Crowe's jealousy is the one thing we have that looks like a motive. If someone else had been killed, we'd know that Crowe was the murderer. Since Crowe himself was the victim, we have to turn the thing around and say that the man Crowe was jealous of, Serena Crowe's lover, is the murderer. I think he must have acted on the spur of the moment, but there's no way of finding out. We can't investigate him unless we know who he is. Since we can't find out—"

"Who says we can't?" Vanya was smiling with malice. Only malice wasn't quite the right word. What was that French word *malin?* Didn't that mean cunning seasoned with malice?

"You know what an *agent provocateur* is?" went on Vanya.

"A policeman who asks a man without a liquor license to sell him liquor. Are you going to chase Serena Crowe to see

104

who gets jealous?"

"Don't be silly. We'll make the police do the work for us."

"How?"

"We'll write a love letter to Serena Crowe and leave it where the police are sure to find it. They'll have to question her about it now her husband's dead in suspicious circumstances, so the whole story of her love affair will come out. And she'll have to tell her lover she's told the police that he had a motive for murdering David Crowe. If he's guilty, he'll be so scared he'll be sure to give himself away."

"Even though he didn't write the love letter?"

"That'll scare him all the more. He'll know that somebody knows about the love affair and is working to unmask him."

"Wouldn't it be a lot simpler just to tell the police what we know about the love affair?"

"Simpler, but not half as much fun. Mrs. Crowe and her lover will have no idea who wrote this letter. They'll be afraid of everybody."

"I almost feel sorry for them."

"Don't. If they're murderers, they deserve it."

"But suppose they're not murderers?"

"Then they'll just have to put up with it until the real murderer is caught."

"If they're guilty, won't they think that whoever wrote the letter is trying to blackmail them?"

"No, because we'll put the letter in a place where the police are sure to find it right away. Once the police know what's in the letter, it has no blackmail value and that will protect us. We don't want anyone to think we're blackmailers. They get killed sometimes."

"Suppose the real murderer is never caught? Won't there be danger of the police arresting Mrs. Crowe or this man?"

"There still won't be enough evidence to convict them, if

they're innocent."

"You hope."

"Well, what is there but our letter? And all it does is establish motive. That's not enough."

"Vanya, I don't believe you've thought this thing through. How can we sign this letter when we don't know who the lover is?"

"It's going to be a two-page letter but the second page with the signature will be missing. It'll be quite clear there is a second page, because we'll break off the first page at the bottom in the middle of a sentence."

"What about handwriting?"

"This letter will have to be typed."

"A love letter? Oh, Vanya, how unromantic! People don't type love letters!"

"I bet some people do, but, whether they do or not, this love letter is going to be typed."

"Perhaps we could put something in the letter about his having hurt his hand so he can't use a pen."

"Corn. And too complicated. It sounds fake. Much better let him just be a simple, unimaginative oaf who types his love letters."

"Or dictates them? Going to put initials in one corner to show which typist in the pool was lucky enough to draw this assignment?"

"On the contrary, we'll be careful to make a few mistakes in the typing to show that he's not the sort who usually does his own typing. He's only doing it this time because it's a love letter and he doesn't want to dictate it to a third person."

"What delicacy! Couldn't he just call in a typist from the pool and say: 'Miss Swivelhips, please write a love letter for me to Mrs. Crowe this afternoon while I play a round of golf'?"

"All right. Laugh. But no matter what you think, Worm, this letter has got to be typed. Handwriting is hard enough to imitate when you know whose handwriting you're imitating, and we don't. Besides, that would be forgery. We can't risk doing anything illegal with the police all over the place."

"How about block capitals?"

"That's only for anonymous letters and blackmail. You'll be suggesting next that we cut printed words out of a newspaper and paste them on a sheet of—"

"—cheap, mass-produced stationery that none of our experts can trace. What's the matter with us, Vanya? This isn't funny. It's serious and here we are laughing."

"It's only the old who take things seriously all the time."

"I hope we'll never be that old."

"Of course we won't. *Nations may disappear . . .*"

"*Heigh-ho! Never fear, we'll be the same.*"

"Here's a pencil and a scratch pad. Let's get to work on the rough draft."

The paper was a kitchen memorandum pad. So there would be no mistake about this the word *Marketing* was printed at the top in red and green and surrounded with a border of fruits and vegetables.

"Vanya, even if the police do question Mrs. Crowe about this letter, we'll never know what she tells them."

"Oh, yes, we will. We'll spend the day in the attic. Listening."

"But your sore throat?"

"It feels all right now."

"But will your mother want you to go out after?—"

"Probably not, but I won't ask her and she won't know where I am. How are we going to start this letter? *Darling* or *Dearest?*"

"Oh, gosh, it's going to be hard for us to write a letter that

107

sounds as if it were written by a grown man to a woman he loves, a woman whom you've never seen and whom I don't like!"

"We won't think about Serena Crowe while we're writing it. You think about your Ideal Man and I'll think about my Ideal Woman."

"What's your Ideal Woman like?"

"Not the way you describe this Crowe person. Come on now, let's get busy! *Dearest* or *Darling?*"

"*Dearest. Darling* is too mushy."

"The kind of love letters that get read aloud in court are always pretty mushy. That's why newspapers print them in full when they can. Give the readers a good laugh."

"I still think *Darling* sounds kind of fake."

"All right then—*Dearest*. Will it be *Dearest Serena* or just plain *Dearest?*"

"Just plain *Dearest*. Then the police will really have their hands full trying to identify the person it's for as well as the person who wrote it. They'll have to do a lot of digging about other people as well as Serena. Heaven only knows what they'll turn up."

"Okay. *Dearest*. Then what?"

Lucinda proffered the pencil. "You ought to write this, Vanya."

"Why?"

"You're a man. You ought to know how men write when they're writing love letters."

To admit inexperience would have been too humiliating. Vanya frowned, clenched his tongue between his teeth for a moment, then took the pencil from her and began to write slowly, speaking the words aloud for Lucinda's benefit as he wrote.

"*Dearest, When we are separated, I die a little . . .*"

"*Separated* is too long and too prosaic. Put *parted* instead."

"Okay. *Parted. You cannot know what these little deaths are like or you would not inflict them upon me.*"

"I don't like *inflict*. Makes Serena sound sadistic."

"Maybe she is."

"But we don't know that. *Impose* would be better."

"*. . . impose them upon me, you who are never cruel.*"

"I rather like that, but, of course, it's derivative."

"How do you mean derivative?"

"Didn't somebody French say *to part is to die a little?*"

"So what? All culture is derivative. The Persians influenced the Greeks and the Greeks influenced the Romans. Let's get on with this. *When I think of that insufferable husband of yours . . .*"

"Oh, no! *Insufferable* is too strong. We've got to be subtle."

"*When I think of that insensitive husband of yours, I realize that this can't go on forever. We must find some way to get rid of him and be together always, just you and me.* That's not bad, is it?" There was a note of surprise in Vanya's voice as if he were pleasantly startled by his own eloquence. "How would you respond if you got a letter like that?"

"Nobody would ever write me a letter like that. I'm too plain," she said with dreadful, self-immolating honesty.

"Just suppose you weren't plain and somebody did write you a letter like that. Would you answer it?"

"Of course."

"What would you say?"

"Oh, I don't know. *Thank you for your nice letter.*"

"*Of the fifteenth inst.?* Really, Worm! I pity any man who ever does write you a letter like that. And now we'd better get going."

"Vanya! Is that all?"

"It's enough if we type triple-spaced on a small sheet of notepaper."

"You forgot to break off in the middle of a sentence."

"Oh, yes." He seized the pencil again. *We must talk the whole thing over. Will you meet me in the*—blank. Break it off right there." He glanced at the kitchen clock. "We'd better go. My mother is usually awake by eight."

"Oughtn't you to leave a note for her? If you don't, she'll be scared stiff when she hears about the murder. She might even tell the police you were missing and they might start hunting for you and that might keep them so busy that they wouldn't pay attention to this letter. Gosh, they might even find us in the attic and ruin all our plans."

"You're right. If I leave a note, she'll just be mad and she won't go to the police the way she would if she were scared."

Vanya scrawled on another slip of paper. *"Feeling fine this morning. Have gone out to ski and may not be back for lunch. Love, Vanya."*

Having tasted the sadistic joys of literary criticism, Lucinda could not give them up at once.

"Well, not *fine. Luncheon,* not *lunch."*

"Oh, for God's sake! How picayune can you get? You stay here and type this while I get my skis."

"Where's the typewriter?"

"Right here." He went into the hall and came back with an Olivetti and some notepaper. "We'll cut off the address at the top. Be as quiet as you can so you don't wake my mother."

Lucinda put the typewriter on the kitchen table and stood up as she typed. Even with only two fingers it didn't take too long to do the few sentences. She didn't have to make any mistakes deliberately. They came naturally.

With a sigh of relief, she sat down on a high stool to wait for Vanya. Would the police trace the typewriter and wonder how Serena Crowe's lover had access to the Radanine house? It didn't matter. What mattered was that they would find out

Serena Crowe had a lover who had an obvious motive for murdering Crowe.

Lucinda wanted to wash the mugs she and Vanya had used but she was afraid to make any more noise. The warmth of the kitchen after the intense cold outdoors was making her nose runny. She slid a hand into the pocket of her parka, hoping to find a piece of tissue. Instead her fingertips touched something hard. She took it out. The little strip of metal she had found in the ashes of the cold hearth at home.

"What have you got there?"

Vanya's voice startled her. The bit of metal fell to the floor. Vanya picked it up. "Where did you get this?"

"I found it this morning in the living-room fireplace."

"What is it?"

"I don't know. It could be almost anything or part of anything. It's awfully hard to identify part of something mechanical, like part of a watch or a typewriter or a car's engine, when you see it out of context. That's why I kept it. I thought we might be able to identify it and . . . Well, couldn't it be a clue?"

"A clue to what?"

"I mean couldn't it have something to do with the murder? I'm pretty sure it wasn't there yesterday afternoon when I watched Martha sweeping ashes out of the fireplace and laying firewood."

"Why didn't you show it to me before?"

"I forgot all about it. Honestly I did."

"You mustn't forget things like that. We must pool all information, or we'll never solve this case." He put the bit of metal in his pocket.

"Can't I have it back?"

"No."

"Why not?"

"It may be dangerous to its possessor. Like the Maltese

111

Falcon or the Fifth Napoleon."

"You mean somebody might murder one of us to get it back?"

"Who knows? Better for me to take the chance rather than you. Now let's go."

Vanya opened the back door. "Oh, Lord!"

"What's wrong?"

"Look."

They could see only six or seven feet ahead of them. The nearest trees were blurred, misty ghosts of their real selves. Beyond, there was no sky, no treetops, no mountains. Only a gray density without light or shadow, form or distance.

Standing in the open doorway, their backs to the kitchen, neither one of them noticed an air current that plucked the note to Vanya's mother from the table, let it drop weightless as a falling leaf to the floor, chivvied it across the linoleum like an invisible kitten and then, with a sigh, let it drift into the narrow crack between wall and refrigerator, where it was lost to view.

"We'll have to go slow," said Vanya. "Take my hand."

They had gone only a little way when Lucinda looked back. She could no longer see Vanya's house. Already the fog had closed in behind them.

"It's like a nightmare I had once," whispered Lucinda. "I was going along a road alone. In front of me, right across the road, there was a wall of mountains, but, with each step I took, the mountains receded, so I could keep going."

"Nothing nightmarish about that."

"Oh, but there was because, after a while, I looked back and then . . ."

"And then what?"

"I saw that, with each step I took forward, another wall of mountains had closed across the road behind me. I could never go back the way I had come."

"What a cockeyed dream!"

"Was it?"

"Well, wasn't it?"

"I don't think so. I think it was symbolic."

"Don't give me that old maidish, neo-Freudian stuff that sees sex in everything!"

"This isn't neo-Freudian symbolism. It's my own personal symbolism. I think the dream was a symbol of time. The past closes behind you and you can never go back."

"You're not the first person to realize that. That's what Stevenson was talking about when he said life is a 'desperate game.' The not being able to go back."

"A murderer must feel that more strongly than anyone else. What could be more irrevocable than murder? It must be awful for the murderer. I never thought of that before. Oh, Vanya, let's not try to catch this one!"

"And give him a chance to kill somebody else?"

"They don't in real life, only in books."

"Oh, yes, they do. That's one reason some psychologists think murder is compulsive. Anything that's repetitive is apt to be compulsive."

They had been inching their way along, blinded by the fog. Now they realized they were near the road because they heard the crunching of snow tires. Yellow fog lights glowed fuzzily for a moment but the car itself was invisible. As it passed them, slowly and cautiously, they realized that the driver was unaware of anyone nearby.

"We'd better not talk now," whispered Vanya. "Even if people can't see us, they might hear us before we knew they were there."

It took time edging uphill silently in deep snow. When they reached the driveway to Crow's Flight, they were panting. They left the driveway and skirted a snowdrift that masked a clump of mountain laurel, so they could come to

113

the closet under the front steps with less chance of being seen from the house.

Lucinda whispered: "Shove your skis in there with mine. You'd better hide there yourself while I scout around and see if the coast is clear."

She was back in a few minutes. "Dr. Willing has taken his wife to the hospital. The others are in the dining room having breakfast and Martha's in the kitchen. We can go through the living room now, if we're quick and quiet."

"The letter?"

"Near the hearth, don't you think? People always burn incriminating letters."

They mounted the steps on tiptoe and slipped through the front door. Firewood was newly laid and the hearth swept clean. Lucinda laid the letter on the hearthstone.

"Suppose someone lights a fire without seeing the letter and it just gets burned up?"

Lucinda switched the letter to the hearth rug. "There! It looks as if someone tried to burn the letter but a gust of wind came down the chimney and blew one page out onto the hearth rug. At least I hope it does. Shall I scorch the edges?"

"It would take too long. Somebody might come." Vanya picked up the hearth brush and swept the last fine dust of ashes onto the rug and the letter. "These ashes are the second page that did burn blown out by the wind along with the first page."

"Why didn't he use another match?"

"It happened after he'd left the letter burning."

"Then let's go. They may finish breakfast at any moment."

They tiptoed across the living room and up the stairs. Vanya stood on the ramp and fumbled along the wall until the hidden panel yielded to his touch.

"Come on!" He dived into the opening. Lucinda followed,

114

pulling the panel into place behind her.

"Home free!" Vanya exhaled audibly. "I feel as if I'd been holding my breath ever since we started out in that fog."

"Not so loud!" Lucinda laid a finger across her lips, whispering close to his ear. "If we can hear Them in here, we know that They can hear us out there. Up you go!"

"Okay."

They were both talking in whispers now. Vanya started to climb the ladderlike crossbeams to the top of the narrow well, Lucinda close behind him. When his eyes were level with the floor of the attic above, he stopped and let out his breath in a gust.

"Move on up!" Lucinda's head was level with his feet. "Or move over. I need another foothold to get up there."

But he stood still. "Worm, somebody else has been here."

"What makes you think so?"

"Look."

Now he did move. Lucinda scrambled up beside him until her eyes were level with his.

"God in Heaven!" Still she kept her voice down to a whisper as she stared about her.

With dust inside and the fog outside only a pallid half-light seeped through the glass in the skylight overhead, but there was enough light to show that every trunk in the attic had been emptied and its contents strewn all over the floor.

Vanya whispered: "It wasn't you who—"

"No, I left everything just as I found it," came Lucinda's answering whisper. "It must've been someone else. Someone who knows just as much about the attic as we do."

Vanya muttered under his breath: "As much . . . or possibly more. . . ."

11

Of the several cars Basil was urged to borrow, he chose the Alcotts' Lincoln, the largest, as likely to be the most comfortable for a passenger with a fractured ankle bone.

After he left Gisela at the hospital, he walked across the street to the garage that had towed his car away for repairs early this morning.

"At least four more hours," the garage man said with stony indifference. "Maybe this afternoon. Maybe tomorrow. Better ring me before you come all the way over here again."

Basil went back to the Alcotts' Lincoln. Soon he was enmeshed in a web of one-way streets that made him feel like a chesspiece that can move only in one direction.

The sun had begun to pierce the fog and, by its light, he saw that the little Hudson River town was keeping up with the times valiantly. A movie house advertised:

INFIDELITY
and
GIRL-KILLERS
For Mature Adults Only

Another movie house proclaimed:

THE TEN COMMANDMENTS
Uncut!
Intact!!
Uncensored!!!

Apparently the earthy, gutsy, bawdy Decalogue was not for immature adults either. . . .

Five minutes later he was in another world, where distant peaks swam in a haze high above the river and the pale winter sunshine sparkled on clean snow. This was the landscape that Bayard Taylor had compared to the Rhine when he stayed at Catskill Mountain House a hundred years ago.

Here and now, all the terrors of last night seemed absurd. Overhead, there was enough watery blue among the clouds to make a pair of Dutchman's breeches and that was supposed to guarantee sunshine for the rest of the day in Greene County. How could he ever have felt as if this road were somewhere off the map, a dark limbo where you groped among fearful things unseen?

It was too early to meet many other cars on the road, but after he had climbed to the top of the first peak and dipped down again into the first ravine where the frozen waterfall glittered, he rounded a curve and discovered a school bus just ahead of him. The way was too narrow for him to pass the bus while it was in motion and of course the law wisely forbade him to pass when it stopped to pick up children waiting for it by the wayside. The children themselves were charming in gaily colored jackets and caps and mufflers, their cheeks as pink as June roses with the cold, but the slow pace was nonetheless infuriating.

Suddenly he came to a fork where a second road snaked off into the woods on his right. He wasn't sure if it was the one he and Gisela had followed last night to Crow's Flight, but it

117

led in that general direction. Without a backward glance at the yellow bus toiling up the next incline at about fifteen miles an hour, he turned into the side road.

What a relief to bowl along at normal speed once more! Even if he was taking the long way round to Crow's Flight, he would feel as if he were getting there more quickly. The way was winding but level here. The unfamiliar car skimmed along like a low-flying bird and his spirits rose. When he came to another fork, he hesitated only a moment, then took a chance on the road to the left. At a third crossroads he bore left again and came to a house that looked like a Swiss chalet. Had he and Gisela passed it in the darkness last night without remarking it?

All the houses they had noticed last night had seemed unoccupied, but there were signs of occupancy here—a car in the driveway, unshuttered windows, white curtains. He would have passed it now without stopping if his glance had not caught the name engraved on one of the two stone pillars at either side of the entrance to the driveway: *Radanine.*

The tall, rusty iron gates stood open. With a flick of two fingers on the power-steering wheel, he turned the car into the driveway and stopped in the half-circle of gravel before the front door.

There was a small, low porch with pillars. Above there was a balcony that ran all around the house, with a carved wooden railing and a sloping roof. Very Swiss. Beyond the house he saw a sunken garden with low hedges and flower beds and fountains all muffled in soft, new-fallen snow. Rather Italian. There were even small, stone figures around a central fountain. They looked as if they had been suddenly frozen in dancing postures. The fat, dimpled face of one of the *amorini* smirked under a cap of icicles. Rather like the Swiss Riviera, someplace in motoring distance of Lugano, where Swiss citizens spoke more Italian than German or French.

Beside the front door was suspended a large, plaster cast of a della Robbia *bambino* and a long, metal bell pull. Basil tugged and heard a bell ring far inside the house, faint but clear. It had the same tone as the cowbells which told you that you were entering Italy before you reached Border Control on the road through the Maritime Alps from Nice to Milan.

The woman who opened the door was almost as tall as Basil himself, but built on more generous lines. She was wearing the fashionable, sleeveless, shapeless dress of the moment that stopped four inches above the knees. Such dresses had a certain decadent style on the fashionable figure of the moment, a figure so skeletal that it suggested a dance of death, but this was a normal, mammalian female in well-fed middle age. The very scale of the opulent curves and quivering cushions of flesh revealed was overpowering. It was rather like looking at a fat little girl seen through an enormously powerful magnifying lens.

"Mrs. Radanine? My name is Basil Willing and—"

"Oh, do come in, Dr. Willing!" The voice was contralto and ripe as the curves of the body, but it was spiced with an accent—not, he thought, a Russian accent. "You stayed at the Swaynes last night, didn't you? I do so want to hear all about it. Is it true that David Crowe was murdered?"

"What makes you think so?"

"The milkman came by this morning. He's just been at the Swaynes' talking to their cook. I got up early to let him in and then I went back to bed."

Basil smiled. "I keep forgetting the country grapevine. In town we depend on TV or newspapers, but here—"

"Here we have native drums! Do come in and have some coffee, won't you?"

In an era when, at least in theory, the poor are no longer poor and the rich no longer rich, houses tend to be similar in size and character and there is only one clue left to the financial status of a householder—upkeep. Even cleanliness is a luxury today in terms of either time or money, and repairing, refinishing and repainting are slipping beyond the reach of many. Of course you can do it yourself, but if you don't want to spend the greater part of your brief time on this planet sanding old furniture and washing windows, you let it go.

Mrs. Radanine belonged in the second category. Basil could not find it in his heart to blame her. To devote one's life to the care of things had always seemed to him an immoral waste.

The living room was clean enough and the furnishings had the haggard charm of an old, worn, shabby elegance, but obviously there was no Martha here to empty scrap baskets regularly and replace flowers in vases when they faded and attend constantly to all the other little things that made Folly's housekeeping so irreproachable.

"You will have coffee?"

"Oh, please don't bother. I just want a word with you." He had already had one cup at Crow's Flight and a second cup with Gisela at the hospital coffee shop, and two cups was all he really wanted any morning.

"But I was going to have some myself and it won't take a moment. I'll bring you a mug. You see, we are mug people."

"So I see." Basil was looking at many rings left by hot mugs on the surface of an old mahogany table.

She was gone before he could make further protest. He hoped she was instant coffee people, too. Mug people usually were. If she wasn't, he was going to be here for a longer time than he had allowed.

His gaze wandered around the room and once again he was reminded of houses on Lake Lugano. The stair that led to a gallery with a carved wooden railing was Swiss in spirit, but the high windows rounded at the top and the marble terrace beyond with balusters shaped like urns were Italianate. So were most of the furnishings in the room—faded green, oyster-white, tarnished gilt—old, gentle colors. Nothing there forced itself rudely on the eye. Everything waited quietly for appreciation.

The hearth was framed in Italian marble. On the mantel shelf there were scattered piles of books: *Poltergeist, Fact or Fancy?* by Sacheverell Sitwell, *Les Maisons Hantées,* by Camille Flammarion, *Mysterious Fires and Lights* by Vincent H. Gaddis . . .

Basil was reaching for that one when Mrs. Radanine returned with a tray.

The coffee was instant. And weak. And lukewarm. There was no sugar, cream or spoon, but it was all served with such an easy amiability that it would have been churlish to resent the omissions.

She lay back on a rococo daybed and smiled as she lifted her mug to her lips. Cheek and neck, shoulders and bosom were so richly curved and creamy that Basil thought of a mound of pearls. Her shift was heavy, unbleached cotton, decorated with cobweb stitching of Mexican embroidery in black, like scrolls drawn in India ink with a finely pointed pen.

Her hair was black, too, straight and oiled and coiled in a great knot low on her neck where it didn't interrupt the classic outline of brow and nape. The dark eyes were large and liquid, the cowlike eyes the ancients attributed to Hera. Radanine sounded Russian, but Slavs didn't look that way. This belonged to the Mediterranean and probably the Eastern Mediterranean.

She put down her mug. "Not quite hot enough." It was not an apology, but a statement of the inevitable. "It won't hurt us to drink it tepid. I don't believe in coddling myself or others. Do you?"

Basil bypassed a question hard to answer within the limits of politeness.

"Now," she went on. "I want to hear all about this affair of David Crowe."

"There's not much I can tell you. The police are at the house. They won't know whether it was a natural death or not until they get the autopsy report. I really stopped by to ask you a few questions about your son. Vanya, isn't it?"

"I will not have him called Vanya! It's a silly nickname. That girl down the road, the Swayne girl, started it. She got it from some story by Tolstoy or somebody."

"You prefer Ivan?"

"I don't like Ivan either. My late husband was Russian. He wanted the boy to be called Ivan. I wanted him to be called Giovanni. I was born in Palermo. And now he is neither Ivan nor Giovanni. He is Vanya and all because of a girl down the road."

"What does he himself want to be called?"

"Something even worse. Johnny. Other boys at school call him that, but to me . . ." Her voice swayed lyrically. "To me he will always be my little Giovanni."

"Then he's half Italian and half Russian? That should be an interesting combination. I have some Russian blood myself, but no Italian."

"Oh, Dr. Willing, Giovanni was born in this country and he's lived here all his life. He's just an ordinary American boy."

"From what I've heard, there's nothing ordinary about him."

"O-oh?" She made it two syllables with a rising inflection. Her heavy eyelids grew heavier and drooped. She looked more Saracen than Italian now. "And what have you heard?"

Basil evaded that issue. "May I see the boy?"

"Why do you wish to see him, Dr. Willing?"

"The girl—Lucinda Swayne—expected him last night. He didn't come. I wondered why."

"But he explained last night. He called the house and told the girl or her father why he couldn't come. He had a sore throat and could not go out."

"Are you sure he didn't?"

"Really, Dr. Willing! You doubt my word?"

"It occurs to me that Giovanni might have slipped out without your knowing anything about it."

"Dr. Willing, my son would never do anything disobedient or deceitful! Never! He has been brought up according to the latest psychological principles."

Basil was tempted to ask: "And what are they this year?" But it would be mere self-indulgence to antagonize a witness who could tell him so much, if she would, so he merely said: "Do you mean Freudian theories?"

"Of course not! Have you never heard of Pavlov?"

"I believe I've heard the name." No point in telling her that he was a psychiatrist. She would talk more freely without that.

She did. Far more freely than he had anticipated. Her Russian husband had known Pavlov and converted her to Behaviorist theories. Her examples of their effectiveness ranged from Watsonian experiments with children to the methods used in Thailand for training apes to pick coconuts. Before long Basil was sneaking glances at his wrist watch.

". . . and that is why I say Giovanni is incapable of mischief. He has been brought up to be independent. He doesn't lean on me. When he was a baby and used to cry, I never picked him up or comforted him or even spoke to him. I just let him cry. Sometimes it would be a long time before he cried himself to sleep. It was hard."

"On him or on you?"

123

"On me, of course. It was good for him. Character building. That's why I did it. I never coddled him. No one can ever call me an overprotective mother."

"No?"

"Well . . ." She smiled. "I try to be."

"Don't fight your natural instincts too hard. All mammalian mothers spend a lot of time, care and affection on their young and by so doing teach the young habits of the species. It's called 'imprinting' nowadays. As an evolutionist, I do not believe that such behavior would have persisted so long if it didn't have survival value."

"But those animal mothers live in the state of nature. We have opted out of the struggle for existence. As members of organized society, we don't have to worry about survival. Society takes care of that for us."

It was time to change the subject. "May I see Vanya? Or rather Giovanni?" Poor boy! It was hardly healthy to change your name so often. Name had so much to do with identity, and identity was always fragile . . . "I'd like to ask him what plans he and Lucinda had for last night—the plans that had to be canceled because of his sore throat."

"But I can't wake him. He's still asleep."

"Are you sure?"

"Of course I'm sure. I told him to let me know the moment he woke, so I could take his temperature. If it's down, he can get out of bed. If it stays down tomorrow and the weather is good, he can go outdoors for five or ten minutes."

"Then there's no hope of my seeing him now?"

"None whatsoever."

Basil sighed and rose. "Let me take this tray out into the kitchen for you—"

"Oh, don't bother! I—"

"No bother at all." Basil wanted to see a little more of the house where Vanya lived. He put the mugs on the tray and carried it through the dining room to the kitchen.

Mrs. Radanine had followed him. "Just put the tray down anywhere."

He hesitated. So many other things had been put down "anywhere" that for a moment he could not see an uncluttered place, but at last he discovered a small one beside the sink.

"Thank you. I'm afraid that—" She stopped. She was staring at a chair in front of the kitchen table.

"Something wrong?"

"Giovanni's ski jacket. It was there, on the back of that chair this morning, when I first got up to let in the milkman. Now it's gone."

Basil caught a note of hysteria. He spoke quietly, hoping to calm her. "Could he have put it on and gone out after you went back to bed?"

"Of course not! He knows he's not supposed to go out this morning, but . . . Excuse me, Dr. Willing. It's time I woke him."

She opened a door. Basil saw an enclosed spiral staircase. Backstairs. He stood at the foot, listening to her quick tread on the stairs, then in the hall above.

"Giovanni! Time to get up now! I—"

The silence was as sudden as if a soundproof door had shut. Then Basil heard quicker steps clattering along the hall and stumbling down the stairs. She surged around the last curve and halted as she saw him still standing at the foot of the stairs.

"Dr. Willing! Giovanni is gone!"

12

FOR A FEW MOMENTS neither Lucinda nor Vanya could move. They could only stand and stare. Outside, the fog was lifting. Suddenly a shaft of chill winter sunshine pierced the skylight and threw into high relief the contents of the trunk nearest their feet.

Lucinda stooped and picked up the feather fan with ivory sticks. The feathers were downy, not very large, white at the centre, shading through off-white to osyter-white to gray at the edge. Fronds of feather drifted to the floor when she opened the fan.

"I wonder what kind of feathers those are." It was no effort to keep her voice down to a whisper now. Only a hushed voice could express her sense of shock. Her fingertips touched the feathers. "Soft as eiderdown."

"Maybe that's what they are," suggested Vanya. "Eiderdown."

Lucinda was looking at a ball dress of changeable silk, pale blue and rose, split down the middle because it had been handled so roughly. "How could anyone do such a thing?"

Vanya smiled wickedly. "I bet you had something like this in mind when I caught you in Folly's room only a day ago.

Remember?"

"That was different."

"Why?"

Her answer came slowly as if she were groping among a confusion of thoughts. "Perhaps some things are all right when you do them yourself, but dreadful when someone else does them. Or . . ."

"Or what?"

"Perhaps I'm changing. Perhaps yesterday I didn't realize how obscene it would look."

"You thought of doing it because you hated Folly and the things were hers," said Vanya. "But whoever owned these things has been dead a long time. Hate doesn't last that long outside Corsica and Kentucky. Why was it done?"

"I suppose these things belonged to David Crowe yesterday and belong to his wife now. Maybe someone hates the whole family. But who? You have to be awfully young to express hate this way."

"Like you yesterday?"

"Like me yesterday. Young or insane. Or perhaps someone was looking for something and flew into a rage when the thing couldn't be found."

"But what would anyone look for among all these old Crowe family things? David Crowe seems to have been the last of the lot and he's dead."

"Mrs. Crowe perhaps? Looking for a will?"

"Nobody keeps a will in a place like this. You leave the original with a lawyer and just have a copy in your safe deposit box."

"Then it's madness."

"Or Mr. Splitfoot."

Lucinda looked at him sidewise.

"I was only kidding," said Vanya.

"Then don't. You didn't hear those raps. I did."

127

She stooped and began folding the old silk dresses, putting them back into the trunk.

"You're not going to repack all this?"

"Of course I am. We can't let all these lovely old things get torn and dirty."

"But it will take hours and —"

Suddenly he was speechless, Lucinda motionless. They could hear footsteps walking on a bare wooden floor. The upper floor? They both glanced toward the well by which they had climbed to the attic, listening for any sound that would mean the panel in the wall was moving. Everything had changed now they had found out that someone else knew about that panel—someone capable of violence.

Lucinda reached out a hand and clasped Vanya's. He helped her to her feet and they stood silent, listening. She let out a gusty breath. The feet were on the stairs now, going down, going away.

Vanya dropped her hand and grinned, as if he were ashamed, as if he wanted to believe he had never been afraid of being caught even for a moment.

Lucinda laid a finger across her lips.

Voices were coming up the stairwell from the lower hall.

"The living room will be the best place."

Vanya looked at Lucinda interrogatively. Without making a sound, her lips shaped a name. "Captain Marriott."

"Shouldn't we wait for Dr. Willing?"

Again Lucinda's lips shaped words: "Cyril Jones, village policeman."

On the side of the mountain nearest the Hudson, names were cosmopolitan, Armenian and Italian, Russian and Jewish, for the river was the original highway from the city. On the other side of the mountain, farther from the river, surnames were eighteenth-century English, and first names tended toward the rococo. Hard-working, simple men who looked like Jims and Joes and Bills answered to Algernon, Reginald or Vivian.

Now Cyril Jones was speaking.

". . . and we can tell him what they say when he gets back. He ought to be here by now. Maybe he's got lost in the woods again." A touch of native scorn for the outsider.

"Well, whatever is holding Dr. Willing up, we can't wait for him." That was Marriott once more. "Jocelyn, you'll take notes."

"Who d'ya wanna see first?" That was Cyril Jones again.

"Women first. After all, the men have alibis and the women don't. I think we might start with Mrs. Swayne. Will you tell her?"

"Sure." Footsteps. "Hey! What's that piece of paper doing on the hearth? It wasn't there earlier this morning."

"Looks as if someone had tried to burn it."

"It's not scorched. Just got some ashes on it."

"Writing?"

"Typing. A letter . . . Well, well! Take a look."

"Huh! No signature, and it's just addressed to *Dearest*. Who's *Dearest?*"

"Maybe Mrs. Swayne can tell us. I'll get her."

Vanya put his lips close to Lucinda's ear and whispered: "Would we hear better to the front of the attic, over the living room?"

Lucinda shook her head. "They might hear us if we moved now. It's all right here as long as they leave the hall door open, I think. Voices come up the stairwell nicely."

She lowered the lid of the nearest trunk carefully and sat down on it as if her legs had suddenly refused to bear her any longer.

Vanya dropped to the floor beside her and sat cross-legged, mouthing another sentence: "This may be fun."

Lucinda shook her head. Her lips were compressed. Her

face looked even paler than usual. Was that just the wan light of the winter sun filtering through dusty panes in the skylight overhead? Or was it something else? Something like fear?

She spoke in a whisper scarcely audible to Vanya.

"If we could get out of here now without being caught, I'd go."

"Why?"

"I don't want to hear this."

"Why on earth not?"

"Oh, Vanya, I'm beginning to feel differently about a lot of things. I don't want to know the secrets of other people's lives any more. I don't even want to know who murdered David Crowe now. It might be somebody we like."

"When did all this start?"

"Just now, I think. When we saw someone had been throwing things around here in the attic. It was so ugly."

"You really are afraid of Mr. Splitfoot, aren't you?"

Lucinda gave him another sidewise look. "If you mean I'm afraid of a disembodied demon, no. But if you mean I'm afraid Mr. Splitfoot is a part of someone we know, yes."

This was a new idea to Vanya. "Split personality?"

Lucinda shook her head. "Nothing quite so pathological. Just Mr. Hyde getting the upper hand of Dr. Jekyll, but each conscious of the other and remembering all the other does. It could happen to anybody. I think it happened to me when I wanted to wreck Folly's room."

Vanya considered. "In that story the best thing is the place where Jekyll finds that Hyde can come when he isn't wanted. Remember? Jekyll glances down at his hand and sees that it has become Hyde's hairy paw without his knowing. Then he knows he's damned and so does the reader."

"Yes, because it's something everyone has experienced. If you give Hyde an inch, he takes an ell and then suddenly he's you and the other you is dead."

Though she spoke in a whisper, Vanya heard emotion in her voice. He opened his mouth to answer her, but he was cut short by another sound from below. The rapid tattoo of high heels, the step of the older generation, female division. No one Lucinda's age wore high heels any more.

They heard Folly's carrying voice, as if she were in the same room.

"Don't apologize, Captain Marriott. I'm glad to do anything I can to help in such dreadful circumstances. I only hope I can help."

Lucinda could visualize her stepmother. It wouldn't be slacks for the police; it would be a dress and wool on such a cold day, the ivory white or the powder pink. The shoes would be claret red with the pink dress or ivory white with the ivory dress and there would be a scarf. Folly liked a scarf to match her jewels and contrast with her dress. Emerald satin and an emerald brooch with the ivory dress. Rose satin and a ruby brooch with the pink dress. She did not subscribe to the outmoded tradition that precious stones were for evening only. With her height and slenderness and her velvet voice she could carry off a certain extravagance in dress that would have been lethal to a dumpy woman with a harsh voice, a woman like Serena Crowe.

At the moment Folly would be seating herself with the grace of a woman who had been trained for the stage—head high, shoulders back, spine straight, ankles crossed, but not knees, hands lying negligently in her lap, palms up. No obscene groping for the seat of her chair with her bottom and no squatting with knees pointing north and south. Actresses were the only women who still knew how to sit, stand and walk. . . .

The sound of her own name drew Lucinda's attention back to the conversation below.

131

". . . any word of Lucinda?" asked Folly.

"Not yet."

"She's such a difficult child! You know she slept all through the fuss when David Crowe's death was discovered."

"She'd had a sedative, hadn't she?"

"Yes, but still . . . There was quite a commotion. It woke everyone else but Lucinda. Even with a sedative I don't believe I could have slept through that hubub. As it was, I was awake for hours afterward."

Liar! I got up at dawn and you were snoring . . .

"Of course after that I overslept and, when I finally woke, Lucinda was gone. It was such a shock on top of everything else."

"Don't worry. She can't have gone far, and I've got two men looking for her. Meanwhile, we must ask you certain questions. Have you and your husband known the Crowes long, Mrs. Swayne?"

"Oh, yes, David Crowe and Frank were at school together and then at Harvard years ago. When David became editor at Alcott and Frank became one of his authors and that must have been fifteen years ago when Lucinda's mother was alive. Of course I haven't known the Crowes that long. I met them when I married Frank four years ago. And Frank hasn't known Serena Crowe that long either. Only since she married David eight or ten years ago."

"Have you seen a great deal of them since you rented this house from them last year?"

"We've seen more of David than Serena. She is very much a city person. She doesn't like the country except in hot weather. David was brought up near Pratt's Landing and he's very much—he was very much attached to this neighborhood. All last autumn he came up alone for weekends during the deer season and later in winter for skiing, and he always stayed with us. Perhaps he came often because he was trying

132

to persuade Frank to buy the house. Serena didn't show much interest until last spring when I did a little altering and decorating. That was when we had finally decided to buy the house."

A little? Lucinda snorted. Just repairing the whole she-bang and building a huge dining room and putting about ten gardeners at work so there was no peace outdoors and she had to spend most of her time at Vanya's house, where things were so much more relaxed. . . .

"What did Lucinda mean by the name 'Mr. Splitfoot'?"

A crystal laugh. "Can't you guess? The cloven hoof. Mr. Splitfoot is an old name for the devil around here. All sorts of curious old ideas linger in mountain country. Where transportation and communication are difficult, people are bound to be conservative."

"Or backward?"

"That depends on the point of view. I can see you're not a Greene County man."

"I'm from Pennsylvania."

"Then you should realize that ecologically these mountains are part of the Appalachian montane block. Perhaps we're part of Appalachia economically as well. There's not much money here."

"Skiing will put an end to that." It was Cyril Jones' voice. "Give us a winter income—winter visitors as well as summer visitors—and real estate values will rise and everything will be different. We might even get light industry to move in."

"I wonder. David used to say that every attempt to estab-lish industry here has failed as if there were a curse on the place. Tanning, quarrying, everything."

A masculine laugh. "Who's responsible for the curse?"

"The Indians, perhaps. They were afraid of the mountains, and, if you look up at them from the Hudson River valley, you can see why. They stand against the sky like a great rampart, wave after wave of smoky blue, remote, enigmatic. Game was plentiful, but the Indians did little hunting here. To spend a night alone here was a puberty rite, a test of manhood. Like the greater mountains of Attica and India, these, too, were known as the Abode of the Gods.

"So . . ." The listeners could hear a smile in her voice. "High, wooded places have always belonged to Pan, the God of Fear. Mr. Splitfoot, who also walks on a cloven hoof, is a medieval version."

Vanya and Lucinda exchanged an uneasy glance.

"Remember what you said," whispered Vanya. "Mr. Splitfoot is just the Hyde part of someone we know."

Lucinda took a deep breath. "Doesn't that make it worse? Much worse . . . ?"

"Mrs. Swayne, did you hear anything last night before you were fully awake and joined the others?"

"No, I slept like a top until I heard the raised voices of the men when they discovered the body."

"Then you didn't hear a bell ring?"

"No."

"And you didn't hear the men talking when they were settling Crowe for the night in the room where he died?"

"No. I dare say they were keeping their voices low so as not to disturb the rest of us."

"Mrs. Swayne, I'd like you to look at part of a letter we found on the hearth."

Vanya and Lucinda exchanged glances again. This time their eyes were bright with irrepressible mischief.

"When did you find this?" For the first time Folly's voice lacked assurance.

"Just now. It was lying on the hearth rug. It looked as if someone had tried to burn it. Someone who was interrupted and had to leave it in the grate hoping it would burn up. Only it didn't. At least this one page didn't. I guess the rest of it did. It must've been some time late this morning, because we went through the ashes on the hearth early this morning and it wasn't there then."

"How could it get on the hearth rug if someone was trying to burn it?"

"When the wind got high enough to blow the fog away, a draught could have come down the chimney and blown it out onto the hearth rug with some ashes. I wish you'd read the letter and tell us what you make of it."

Silence stretched. If Folly had not spoken when she did, Lucinda could not have borne it another moment.

"Obviously a love letter, but I have no idea who wrote it or for whom it was intended. Have you?"

"We were hoping you might be able to guess from something in the letter itself."

"I don't like to guess. I might get some innocent person into trouble."

"I'd understand that feeling in ordinary circumstances, but these circumstances aren't ordinary. We're looking for a murderer."

"How could a silly letter like this help you to find a murderer?"

"It might give us a motive."

"I see." Folly's usually smooth voice faltered. It was apparent to the listeners that she was fighting for self-control. When she spoke again, she had achieved it. "This puts me in a difficult position."

"Why?"

"I have some reason to believe that the letter may have been intended for me."

"What reason?"

"David Crowe was not happy in his marriage. I've told you already that he came here frequently without his wife, but I didn't tell you that there were several occasions when I . . .

135

Well, let's just say that sometimes I found his attentions embarrassing."

"Did you mention this to your husband?"

"Oh, no. And I hope you won't do so. The fewer people who know, the less disturbing for everybody. I'd like Frank to go on remembering David as an old and trusted friend and thinking of me as a wife whom no other man would dare approach. Don't you understand? If Frank knew about this, he would always wonder if I had done anything to encourage David, and I don't want that. Divorces are caused by husbands or wives who insist on easing their consciences by telling all—a frightful mistake. If they'd just kept their mouths shut, everything would have been all right, but once the slightest doubt arises in a marriage, nothing is ever the same again. It's bad enough to wreck your marriage for the sake of a man you love, but just think how intolerable it would be to wreck your marriage for the sake of a man you didn't love. I didn't love poor David so . . . the less you say to anyone else about this, the better."

"I'm sorry I have to ask these questions, but I must."

"I understand all that and that's why I'm answering you so frankly."

"Do you think that Crowe might have written you a letter like that?"

"It does sound preposterous, but he might. He was awfully persistent."

Lucinda winced as she caught the note of complacent sexual vanity in Folly's voice.

"Did he write you other letters like this?"

"Never."

"Then your only reason for thinking he may have written this to you is your awareness of his . . . er . . . romantic interest in you?"

Vanya's lips formed the word "romantic" and he rolled his

eyes to Heaven. Lucinda knew how he felt. How could men well over forty like David Crowe have romantic feelings for anyone? Wasn't that the age when they were supposed to concentrate on careers and children? In Japan, didn't men that age start reading the Holy Sutras to prepare themselves for their descent into the Land of Yomi? As the Japanese chronicles said: *To be old and wise is well, but some men are old and foolish.* . . . Apparently David Crowe fell into this unfortunate category.

"Who else in this household might have written such a letter?" That was Marriott's voice once more.

"I don't believe there is anyone else who would. Bradford Alcott is old and ill. I do not see him in the role of an adventurous or ardent lover. And of course my husband wouldn't write such a letter to anyone but me, and the wording of this letter doesn't fit our relationship. We're never separated, or 'parted,' as the letter puts it."

"Could Mr. Crowe have written the letter to some other woman?"

Folly was astonished. "You mean to his wife?"

"No, it doesn't sound like a letter from a husband to his wife. What about Mrs. Alcott?"

"Oh . . . Well, of course, Mrs. Alcott does have a rather superficial attraction for some men . . . if they care for Irish blarney and a rather disheveled appearance, but she wasn't David Crowe's type at all and she must be years older than he was."

"Thank you, Mrs. Swayne. I don't believe we need question you any further at the moment."

A chair scraped. "I do hope you won't have to tell anyone else about this. I mean about David's letter to me."

"There's no reason to tell anyone else about that unless we discover that the letter has something to do with Crowe's death."

"How could it?"

"Don't you realize that you have given your husband a classically traditional motive for murdering Crowe?"

"Oh, but that's ridiculous. Frank might knock another man down in hot blood, but he'd never concoct an elaborate plot, building up a Gothic atmosphere to make it look as if the man he'd killed had been frightened to death."

"If this was murder, it may not have been an elaborate plot. The murderer may have been an opportunist who saw his chance and took it on the spur of the moment after the Gothic atmosphere had been built up largely by Crowe himself and your stepdaughter. What about the Mr. Splitfoot bit? Has it occurred to you that someone else may have prompted Lucinda to play a prank on the assembled company?"

"She wouldn't need prompting, but I can't imagine how she could manage to make those raps respond to her voice when we were all watching her."

"But if she could she would?"

"Oh, yes. She's a mischievous child. Perhaps it's my fault."

"How could it be your fault?"

"I don't like her. Don't look so shocked! You want the truth, don't you? I know children need to be loved, and when I married Frank I was resolved to love Lucinda, but I couldn't. Love is not something you can turn on and off like a spigot. I've been generous to her with my money and time and things like that, but I cannot make myself love her. It's unfortunate, because children can always tell. Old men are the only people who can be made to accept counterfeit love as the real thing. The poor dears are easy to deceive because they do so want to be deceived. They're desperate. But children don't want to be deceived. They want the real thing or nothing."

This time it was Vanya's hand that crept out in search of Lucinda's. He found hers cold and shaky.

"Have you any idea why you feel this way about your stepdaughter?"

"She'll never answer that!" whispered Vanya.

But she did. Perhaps it was a relief to speak so unreservedly for once to men she would probably never see again when this was over.

Her clear, cool voice was defiant. "The role of a second wife isn't easy, especially if the first wife is dead. Who can compete with the dead? I've always been jealous of Frank's first wife and everything that belonged to her, including Lucinda. I have no children of my own to make it easier. So I smile and smile and I'm a villain still in my heart. I can't help it. On the surface everything is smiling, but underneath there's been a cold war between me and that girl ever since I married her father. Perhaps I didn't try hard enough . . . Is there anything else, Captain Marriott?"

"That's about it, Mrs. Swayne. Thank you. Will you please ask Mrs. Crowe if she can see us now?"

The staccato tap of high heels came up the stairs and faded down the corridor. A door closed softly.

Lucinda snatched her hand away from Vanya. "We'll have to tell the police we wrote that letter now! Folly's using the letter to make it sound as if Daddy had a motive for killing David Crowe. Is that just vanity or stupidity or—"

"Sh-sh!" Vanya laid a hand over her mouth.

Cyril Jones was speaking. "Suppose Mrs. Swayne left her bedroom during the night. Would the stepdaughter sleeping in that same room hear her in spite of the sedative?"

"That's something we'll have to ask the young lady when we find her."

Vanya looked inquiringly at Lucinda. She shook her head

violently and opened her lips to speak, but Vanya stopped her with an almost inaudible whisper: "Here comes someone else."

The step that reached the listeners in the attic suggested a slow shuffle in flat slippers.

"Sorry to disturb you, Mrs. Crowe, but it's nearly noon." This was Marriott.

"I know." The answering voice was furred with drowsiness. "I know. I was awake in the night. I took something I had with me to make me sleep afterward. I'm still sleepy." There was a sound of yawning.

"Would you like coffee?"

"That would be wonderful."

"I'll see to it . . ." Footsteps receding. They must have been Jones' steps, for Marriott's voice went on:

"Try the sofa. Make yourself comfortable."

"Thanks. I must apologize for the way I look. I didn't even brush my hair. I feel awful."

"We'll try not to keep you too long. . . . Oh, here's coffee."

As soon as the clatter of cups and saucers had subsided, Marriott said: "Mrs. Crowe, can you suggest any reason why anyone might want to kill your husband?"

"I thought it was a natural death."

"We can't be sure until we get a medical report, and we have to consider every possibility."

"I can't imagine anyone wanting to kill him. He didn't lead the sort of life where you make that kind of enemy."

"Did you see or talk to anyone after you went upstairs to your bedroom last night?"

"Not really. I said good night to Folly and Ginevra in the upper hall and closed my door and went straight to bed. I thought David would be up in a little while. I even left a light for him. It was still burning when they woke me in the

140

middle of the night to tell me that he was dead."

"Did you hear any sounds during the night?"

"Oh, no. The last thing I heard as I dropped off to sleep was the murmur of men's voices downstairs. I suppose they were making their silly plan to trap the ghost or the trickster or whatever they thought it was. After that I slept right through until they woke me."

"Have you any explanation of the Mr. Splitfoot business?"

"You mean when the girl clapped her hands three times and there were three raps in response? No, I haven't. I suppose it was a trick, but I can't see how it was worked."

"Who do you think worked the trick?"

"The girl, or course. Who else? She's a sly little thing and obviously bored up here with no companions her own age except that awful Russian boy down the road."

Vanya winked at Lucinda and she winked back.

"How well do you know the Swaynes?"

"Not too well. David saw more of them than I did."

"Mrs. Crowe, we'd like you to look at this letter we found on the hearth rug. It breaks off in the middle of a sentence and there's no signature. Can you suggest who might have written it?"

Silence. A rattle of paper.

"It reads like a love letter, but I have no idea who would write a letter like that or whom it would be meant for."

"Liar!" whispered Vanya. "How can she be involved in a whatchamacallit—sordid intrigue—and not admit that the letter might be addressed to her?"

Captain Marriott seemed to have a similar idea. "You don't think it may have been written to you?"

"Of course not! David and I had an ideal relationship. Perfect love and trust. Everyone knew that. No one would even think of addressing such a letter to me."

Vanya shook his head in silent disgust.

141

"Then you can't even guess who wrote the letter? Or whom it was meant for?"

"I suppose it must have been meant for Folly. Poor, dear Ginevra is too old for that sort of thing and Lucinda's too young. But Folly's about the right age."

"And the man who wrote it? According to the letter, he is someone here now."

"Then it just has to be Bradford Alcott, doesn't it? If Folly was the woman, it couldn't have been Frank, because this is not a husband's letter to a wife, and it couldn't have been my David because he was so utterly devoted to me. He used to become quite ridiculously jealous if I even looked at another man."

Again a note of complacent sexual vanity made Lucinda wince.

"David and I had a rather special relationship," went on Serena. "Ten years ago when we were just married he was driving when I told him that he shouldn't because he'd had too much to drink. But he would drive and he crashed and I went through the windshield. I nearly died. I was in the hospital for months. My face was . . . chopped meat. You can see all the little scars now in bright sunlight where they fixed me up and made me presentable, but they couldn't make me what I had been before it happened. I don't look much like a professional model now, do I? But I was once. My face was my fortune. David felt simply horrible. He never got over it. Now are you beginning to understand that our relationship was sort of special?"

"Yes, I can see what you mean," Marriott answered her. "That would be quite a special sort of hold on a husband. I believe that—"

There was a crash of falling china. "Oh, dear!" A gasp. "Excuse me, please . . . I must . . . the bathroom. . . ."

Footsteps hurrying away.

142

"Let me help." More footsteps. A dreadful retching sound. A door closing. Footsteps returning slowly.

"Is she sick?" There was wonder in Marriott's voice.

"Very. All over the downstairs bathroom." That was Jones. "I've asked the cook to look after her. No one else was handy."

"Maybe that sleeping pill she had last night upset her stomach?"

"Or one of our questions?"

"They were pretty mild questions. I can't understand such a violent reaction."

Footsteps were running down the stairs. A door opened.

"What have you been doing to poor Mrs. Crowe?" Ginevra Alcott seemed furious.

"Not our fault, Mrs. Alcott. We were questioning her quietly enough when suddenly she vomited. We're still wondering why."

"Perhaps your questions were more important to her than you realized."

"That's one of the things we're beginning to suspect."

"Are you going to question me now?"

"You're next on the list."

"Then please get it over with. What do you want to know?"

"For one thing: can you explain this letter we found on the hearth rug this morning? Apparently someone tried to burn it. We don't know who wrote it or to whom it was addressed."

"Let me put on my glasses. . . . Did you show this to Serena Crowe just before she collapsed?"

"Yes. Why?"

"Her husband wrote it. She must have guessed."

"What makes you think her husband wrote it? Have you seen the letter before?"

"No, but . . . I suppose I'll have to tell you now. I hope it won't be necessary for you to tell anyone else. David Crowe was in love with me. I thought I'd convinced him that it was hopeless, but apparently I hadn't. If Serena saw this letter last night . . . if she realized that David was still in love with me . . ."

"Are you suggesting that she was jealous enough to kill her husband?"

"I won't go that far. We're not even sure he was killed yet, are we? But this letter does give her a rather obvious motive, doesn't it?"

13

LUCINDA, ALL ATTENTION concentrated in her ears, caught the note of assurance in Ginevra's voice. The voice made it easy to recall the serene arrogance of the haggard, once-beautiful face and still-beautiful eyes. Lucinda spared a moment to consider the harsh inequalities of adult life.

Like a card game. At birth you were dealt a hand. That, far more than skill in playing, determined your fate. Ginevra had had such a splendid hand. Beauty, health, wealth, position, brains, education, even charm. What did she lack? There must be something. No one player could hold all the court cards. That was against the rules of the game, or the law of probability, or something.

It came to Lucinda with sudden conviction that Ginevra had missed the most important card of all—a heart. Some people might argue that the heart is more a liability than an asset, but is it really? The experiences of the heartless are so limited. It is hate that is blind. Love may miss a flaw here and there, but hate misses beauty everywhere.

Ginevra was trying to explain what she had said about David Crowe and herself. "This sort of happens because my husband is so much older than I am. . . ."

How heartless the words sounded. Why had she married him if she felt this way about him under all the elegance and grace and charm that she deployed so adroitly wherever she went? She didn't need money or power. She had those already from her own family. Or so Folly had said once to her husband in Lucinda's hearing. Was it impossible for Ginevra to have too much power?

". . . and you didn't hear any sound during the night?"

"None whatsoever. I doubt if any of the women could have heard a sound from the room where David Crowe died. It's off by itself at the end of the upper hall, facing the stairs. It's a corner room, and two of its walls are outside walls. The third wall divides it from the upper hall and the fourth from Lucinda's bathroom. We all had our doors shut. The men downstairs were far more likely to hear a noise in that room than we were."

"Why?"

"Have you studied the plan of the house?" Ginevra sounded like a schoolteacher: *Have you done your homework?* "The fireplace in the bedroom where David died is in the same chimney as the living-room fireplace. If you know anything about old houses, you know what that means. A conversation in that bedroom may be heard in the living room below.

"And that's not all. When central heating was put in this house long ago, some odd devices were used that would be scorned by a modern heating engineer. They heated the ground floor with ducts from a hot-air furnace in the cellar, but upstairs they just put open registers or grilles in the floors without ducts, knowing that heat rises and hoping that this would keep rooms upstairs reasonably warm. There's still a register in the ceiling of this room which leads through the floor of the room above, the haunted room. Haven't you noticed?"

"No. Where is it?"

"Right here."

A stirring, scraping of chairs, footfalls out of step with one another. A sudden silence.

"There. See the fancy rococo grille? Right in front of the fireplace. It's in shadow between two exposed beams, so I suppose you might not notice it unless you were looking for it."

"Why is there no light from above?"

"There must be a rug over the grille upstairs—probably the hearth rug of the upstairs fireplace."

"Why don't you go upstairs, Cyril, and see what's there."

Footsteps on the stairs. Lucinda and Vanya lay still as mice in a wainscot.

"Why do you suppose the register is so close to the fireplace?" That was Marriott's voice again.

"So it will carry warmth from the fire upstairs as well as warmth from the heating system. Isn't it silly to have a thermostat in this room? Every time they light a fire in here, the room gets so hot that the thermostat shuts off and the rest of the house freezes."

"They should have the thermostat in the hall," said Marriott.

"They should install a thermostat in every room!" retorted Ginevra.

"But that would be far more expensive and—" Marriott's voice stopped as if he had suddenly realized that when you were talking to Ginevra Alcott you were talking to someone who had never been forced to regard expense as an obstacle and who could not imagine what life was like for those who did. Lucinda wondered what it would do to you to live a life in which nothing you really wanted was ever denied to you. . . .

"It was a hearth rug, Captain."

"Okay, Cyril. The light's coming through now. Can you hear me all right up there?"

"Sure thing."

"If this were my house, I'd have all these holes in the upstairs floors filled in," said Marriott. "I like privacy."

"Oh, most of them were filled in long ago," said Ginevra. "The grilles were removed and the holes boarded over and covered with carpet in every upstairs bedroom. The whole upstairs is heated by ducts to the furnace now."

"Then why wasn't this one filled in at the same time?"

"This one is in the haunted room, the room that was locked up for two generations. Had you forgotten? No one thought that room would ever be used again, so no one bothered with it. Of course when people were here in the living room, there were no noises from that empty room above to remind people that the open grille was still there."

"But in all that time anything that was said down here in the living room could be heard up there in the haunted room?"

"I suppose so, but that would hardly matter when no one wanted to go into the haunted room and it was kept locked up all the time."

"No one? How can you be sure? Let's put it this way: anyone who could get hold of a key to that room, and who was not afraid of ghosts, could hear anything that was said in the living room at any time."

"I got an impression last night that everyone was rather afraid of the haunted room even though they didn't care to admit it in so many words."

"Perhaps some were less afraid than others."

"What do you mean?"

"There's been a good deal of storm and strife in this house according to the story Crowe told last night. I can't help wondering if it may not have been caused by things that were overheard."

"What a frightful idea!" But Ginevra's voice belied her words. She didn't think it was frightful. Her voice was fruity with enthusiasm as she went on: "You mean one sister was with her lover in the room where he died later and the other sister, creeping down here when they thought she was asleep in her own room, heard everything?"

"Wouldn't that explain a crime of jealousy if there was one? Hearing is believing. Much more impact than hearsay."

"No wonder that room is haunted!" A chair scraped again. "If you don't need me for anything further . . . ?"

"Not for the moment, Mrs. Alcott, but will you be kind enough to ask your husband if he can give us a few moments now?"

"Brad? . . . Oh, yes, of course. . . ." There was a snag in her voice as if it had caught on something rough.

Vanya shifted his cramped position gingerly to make as little noise as possible while he stretched his legs. Lucinda realized that one of her feet had gone to sleep. She rolled on her side so she could bend one knee and began to massage the offending foot. The pins-and-needles feeling was kind of fun—not pain, not pleasure, but something between the two.

"I—I'm afraid there's nothing I can tell you—"

Lucinda stopped massaging her foot. She had not heard Bradford Alcott come into the room, but that was his voice, and how different it was from Ginevra's voice. Ginevra assumed a superiority to other people, but, if you listened closely, you could hear a faint tremor of self-doubt underneath her assurance. Alcott had no doubts about his superiority. He knew.

It wasn't the sort of superiority that is based on contempt for other people. Contempt implies some form of response to others and Alcott was totally unresponsive. Underneath a thin skin of conventional propriety he maintained a single-minded boredom for everyone in the world save possibly himself, and Lucinda had an odd feeling that he didn't care very much for himself either.

Why hadn't she realized this before? Was it because, until now, his rather pleasant appearance had distracted her from the full impact of his voice? But now she heard the voice alone, disembodied, it revealed itself as one long yawn of utter ennui made audible.

Perhaps that was one of the advantages of eavesdropping: it isolated the voice from everything else. For wasn't the voice the most revealing thing among all external aspects of personality?

She wrenched her attention back to what Alcott was saying. It was hard to keep attention fixed on words dragged out so languidly.

"I haven't the slightest idea who wrote the letter. If it was written to my wife, I suppose it could have been written by either Swayne or Crowe.

"Don't misunderstand me. I am not suggesting that my wife is indiscreet, but she is romantic. Everyone we meet soon realizes that I am a dying man and therefore an inadequate husband. This exposes my wife to all sorts of advances." A hint of irony came into his voice. "The kind of thing that is regarded as an insult by a young woman and as a compliment by an old woman. My wife is just old enough to be gentle with any man who smiles at her."

Never before had Lucinda heard anyone speak of his own imminent death. Was it always like this at the end? Did you have to sit still and calm knowing that some time soon, in a year or a month or a moment, perhaps when it was least expected, you would suddenly cease to be a part of the world and it would go on quite happily without you? Was that why Alcott seemed so inhumanly detached and self-centered? Had she mistaken despair for arrogance?

She looked at Vanya with wide eyes and whispered: "Do you suppose it takes courage to be old?"

Vanya shook his head violently. He wasn't answering her question. He was just warning her not to risk prolonged whispering.

"I'm sorry." That was Marriott's voice. "Heart condition?"

"That's one name for it. My father died of it. I know exactly what to expect, only I don't know when or where. This has been going on for two years and I'm tired of it. Almost a drop-that-other-shoe feeling . . . What else did you want to ask me?"

"Which man is more likely to have written such a letter? Swayne or Crowe?"

"I really can't say with only the letter to go by. It's extraordinary how much all men are alike when you get down to the erotic level of experience. It seems to be the bedrock of personality where individuality ends. That's why I suppose all love letters are full of clichés. Certainly this one is. On the basis of the letter alone, I'd say that neither Crowe nor Swayne could have written it. They were both far too intelligent."

Vanya looked furious. "Clichés, indeed!" he muttered.

"When you came down here with the others last night after leaving Crowe upstairs, did you hear any sounds at all from upstairs before you heard the bell ring?"

"No, just the bell."

"What were the last words Crowe spoke when you and the others left him alone in the haunted room?"

"I've tried to remember that since all this happened. Unfortunately the only thing I can recall doesn't quite make sense, so I must have been mistaken."

"And that was?"

"Willing had almost reached the door. I was halfway there

151

and I looked back. Swayne was still standing beside Crowe. He clapped Crowe on the back and Crowe muttered something I didn't quite catch. What it sounded like is absurd." A faint chuckle tinged with embarrassment. "It sounded like Tobruk."

"Tobruk?"

"Doesn't the word mean a thing to your generation? That does make me feel old. It was a battle in North Africa. Of course Crowe wouldn't have been talking about that, so he must have said something else, but what it was I cannot tell you."

They didn't keep Alcott much longer. As soon as his footsteps receded, Cyril Jones said: "We must ask Swayne himself just what it was Crowe said."

There was a silence, then Marriott's voice. "Too bad witnesses have to be questioned one right after another."

"Why?"

"You don't have time to digest what each one says before you go on to the next. So they overlap and blur together and— "Oh, come in, Mr. Swayne. We were just going to send for you."

"I thought you'd be wanting me now. You've seen everyone else. I hope the morning has brought daylight in more senses than one."

"This morning has brought only fog in every sense. We've found what seems to be a love letter, typewritten, oddly enough, and addressed simply to 'Dearest.' The last part of it is missing, so there's no signature. No one we've talked to knows who wrote it and there are no clues in the letter itself. It could have been written to anyone by anyone. Here it is. Can you make anything of it?"

After a few moments the listeners heard Swayne's voice again. "I'm afraid I can't say anything except that I did not write it myself, and I doubt very much if either Crowe or

Alcott wrote it. The wording of the letter doesn't sound like either one of them. Brad is obviously too old and ill for this sort of thing, and the letter itself sounds pretty immature for a man like David Crowe."

Vanya was indignant. "I don't see anything immature about it!"

"Neither do I," Lucinda whispered back. "What's more, Mrs. Crowe did have a lover. I heard her husband accusing her. Why won't any of them admit it? Don't they know? Or are they just covering up for her?"

Marriott was speaking again. "There seems some doubt about whether or not you intended to buy this house. Did you?"

"Oh, yes. That was clearly understood between David and myself. I wouldn't have made the alterations otherwise. I had an option to buy in my year's lease."

"The ghost story didn't discourage you?"

"No, it rather added to my interest. What I believe is called a conversation piece these days."

"We've learned that there is an open register in the ceiling of this room that goes through the floor of the so-called haunted room above where Crowe died. It seems as if most sounds would come through such a register, even if it were covered with a rug. Do you recall hearing any sounds from up there, however slight, after Crowe was left there alone last night?"

"No, I don't recall a thing. Of course we were talking most of the time and I don't suppose any of us would have noticed a slight sound."

"We've been told that just before Crowe was left alone in the haunted room last night he said something to you under his breath that was inaudible to the other two men. Do you remember what it was?"

"Let's see if I can remember . . . Willing and Alcott were

almost at the door. I took a last look at things on the table to make sure everything was there and I think I put a hand on Crowe's shoulder . . . Yes, I did. And I said . . . What the hell did I say? Oh, I know! I said: 'Going to read?' He had the book open on his knee, but he shook his head and muttered something. . . . What was it? Oh, yes. He shook his head and muttered: 'No, to brood.' I thought he meant to brood over some business worries. Now I'm not so sure, but that's what I thought at the time. I smiled and lifted my hand in a sort of salute and followed the others out of the room. God, I had no idea that was the last time I'd see him alive. . . . Not too helpful, I'm afraid, is it?"

"I hardly expected it to be, but there's always a chance that some little thing will prove significant. I've even wondered about Mrs. Crowe's sudden attack of nausea this morning. We weren't questioning her about anything important. I suppose it could be just delayed shock. . . ."

"Nausea can be a symptom of almost anything," said Swayne. "Including pregnancy!" Obviously this was a new idea to Marriott. "That might have all kinds of ramifications. Inheritance . . . paternity . . ."

But they were not destined to explore such ramifications at that moment.

Footsteps clattered outside and a door crashed open.

"Oh, Frank! I'm so sorry to bother you at a time like this, but is Giovanni here? No? Oh! My poor darling! He's disappeared! He's been kidnaped or murdered!"

"Oh, hell!" whispered Vanya. "Didn't she find my note?"

"Dr. Willing stopped at my house on his way here and that was when I found Giovanni was gone. We looked everywhere. Tell them, Dr. Willing!"

"Vittoria, please!" said Swayne. "Don't talk so loud. You'll disturb Serena."

"And why shouldn't she be disturbed when my

Giovanni—"

"If only she wouldn't call me Giovanni!" muttered Vanya.

"Serena isn't well. If you'll just take it easy, I'll ask Lucinda if she knows where Vanya is."

They heard his steps coming up the stairs. They heard his voice in the upper hall. "Folly, do you know where Lucinda is?"

"No, I haven't seen her for hours. Isn't she in her room?"

"Let's look. . . . No, she isn't. Come to think of it, I haven't seen her all morning, have you?"

"No, I haven't. Do you suppose she's gone out?"

"Let's check her skis."

Footsteps going downstairs.

Soon Vanya's mother was in full cry. "Lucinda is missing, too? Oh! Oh! Oh! Those poor little ones! So trusting! So helpless! Babes in the woods! They'll freeze to death. Or break their legs. Why was skiing ever invented? And with a murderer at large—probably a homicidal maniac—"

"Let's not assume the worst until we've made sure they're not near the house," said Marriott.

"If they were near the house, they'd come if we called. Giovanni! *Lucinda!* GIOVANNI! You see, Captain Marriott? No answer. You must organize a search party. At once!"

"We can't just sit here," whispered Lucinda. "What shall we do?"

"Nothing. Unless we want them to find out about this hiding place and ruin it forever."

"But . . . this is awful!"

"Yes, isn't it?"

14

BASIL WILLING STAYED with Mrs. Radanine a little longer when the others went to search the woods. Though he managed to maintain an appropriate air of sympathetic concern, he felt as if he were watching an overdirected play. Vittoria was beside herself with fear, yet it was quite obvious that another part of her personality was having the time of its life. She was not unaware that she was the centre of the stage.

She had run her fingers through her hair and the sleek, black knot on the nape of her neck had uncoiled, giving her a look of disheveled grief. She had wrenched the low neck of her Mexican dress so that it had ripped across one shoulder. All she needed now was a touch of ashes to express mourning in its most ancient form.

The effect was too much like a ritual to seem real. Basil had to remind himself that this woman's son and the Swaynes' daughter were missing in a neighborhood where a man had died in peculiar circumstances the night before and that it was just possible they might be in some real danger.

Vittoria's outcry had drawn Folly and Ginevra from upstairs. Now each was offering sympathy in her different way.

Ginevra was all soothing volubility and vague reassurance, the caressing Irish lilt in her voice more pronounced than ever. Folly was offering practical suggestions.

Was it just a difference in manner that made Folly seem so cool? Or was her sense of decorum so outraged by this emotional explosion that she was trying to instill a little of her own self-control into Vittoria by example? It was only too easy for Folly to keep cool in the circumstances. She had none of the feelings for her stepdaughter that Vittoria had for her son.

"Why don't you lie down and rest?" urged Folly. "Captain Marriott and the other men are searching the woods. They're sure to find Giovanni. He's only been missing a little while. He can't have gone far."

"Little while!" Vittoria's opulent bosom heaved and she threw out her ample white arms as if she were embracing grief. "I have not seen him since last night, and he was ill then with fever—too ill to go out. That was fourteen hours ago! Or is it sixteen? You call that a little while? Do you? Do you?"

"He's probably not alone," said Folly. "Lucinda is sure to be with him, since they are both missing. If there has been a skiing accident, only one is likely to be hurt. The other can come and tell us."

"A-a-ah!" It was more like singing than wailing do, fa, sol, with a vibrato on the last soprano note. "That girl!" The woodwinds were taking up the theme now. "She is the one who leads my Giovanni astray. He is innocent as the Paschal lamb, an angel, a saint, brought up according to the latest scientific principles and—"

This was too much for Folly. "Who ever heard of a saint brought up according to the latest scientific principles? Really, Vittoria! You know perfectly well that Vanya is a mischievous boy who—"

157

"He is not mischievous and his name is not Vanya! It is the girl who calls him that. His name is Giovanni."

Folly lit a cigarette and exhaled the first fine feather of smoke. "He told me his name was Jack."

"Are you suggesting that I do not know the name of my own son?"

Folly changed her tactics. "Vittoria, dear Vittoria, do come upstairs and leave all this to the men. I'll make you a cup of tea with a little brandy in it. Your poor, dear nerves are all raw and quivering and no wonder. . . ."

It was obvious that Folly's nerves were not raw and quivering, that Lucinda's disappearance had not disturbed her at all. Basil decided that he liked her better when she was being astringent with Vittoria, but apparently Vittoria could not tell the difference between real compassion and its counterfeit. Protesting, weeping, still voluble, she allowed herself to be led upstairs with Folly's arm around her.

Ginevra looked at Basil. "Is Bradford really out in the woods searching with the other men? He shouldn't have gone. Suppose he gets separated from the others and has an attack when he's alone and there's no one to give him his medicine quickly? He might die in seconds."

"I didn't realize his condition was so serious."

"Well, it is." She sighed. "It's been going on for years now, of course. If he takes life calmly and keeps his medicine handy, he manages to exist, but it's not really living, is it? The possibility of an attack is always hanging over him and I don't like him to be left alone. If he had a severe attack, he'd need someone to give him the medicine. He might not be able to do it himself. Isn't it strange how we never know consciously what is going on in our own bodies? We may feel perfectly well and on top of the world and all the time the first little cancerous cell may be starting to spread or the first accretion of cholesterol to coat the inside of our arteries. If only these things were as painful as a toothache in the beginning, we might have a chance of doing something before it was too late."

"If you'd been with us last night, I don't suppose you would have wanted your husband to join in our little experiment in the haunted room."

"No, I wouldn't. I asked him this morning if he didn't think he had been unwise. Suppose that when you drew cards to see who should spend the night in the haunted room, the lot had fallen on him instead of David Crowe? Would he have gone through with it? He said he would. He was convinced that there was no danger of anything happening that could upset him, because he didn't believe in ghosts or poltergeists or anything of that sort. He thought then that the whole thing was some silly hoax. It never occurred to him that anyone was going to die."

"Any sign of them yet?" Captain Marriott was standing in the front doorway, Swayne and Alcott just behind him. "I thought I heard a cry."

"The boy's mother having hysterics," said Ginevra. "Folly finally got her upstairs."

"Oh . . ." Marriott stamped on the doormat, loosening some of the snow from his boots. "I've got a dozen men searching the woods now, some troopers and some locals from the village, but I still think it's too soon to call this a disappearance and send out a full alarm. They're both young and their skis are missing. We found some tracks of two skiers who left the Radanine house together and got as far as the road. We haven't been able to trace them farther because tire tracks on the road have obliterated the ski tracks, but we'll find where they left the road eventually. They're probably somewhere close by having the time of their lives in the snow and not realizing what a storm they've kicked up here."

Or realizing it very well and enjoying themselves all the

more, thought Basil.

"I still think they're most likely to be in the woods between here and the Radanine house," said Swayne.

"We did search there," objected Alcott.

"But not thoroughly enough. We should search again."

"Okay, Mr. Swayne," said Marriott. "You take over the east side of the road to the Radanine house and Mr. Alcott can—"

"Mr. Alcott can't," said Ginevra sharply. "He's looking tired already."

"I can at least walk down the road to the Radanine house," suggested Alcott in his weary voice. "Mild exercise is supposed to be good for me. Remember?"

"I'll walk with you," said Ginevra.

There was a flash of impatience in Alcott's eyes, the only time Basil had ever seen his lethargy stirred. But it was only a flash. When he spoke a moment later, his voice was level as ever. "How kind of you, my dear. Shall we go now?"

How hard for a man who had once shouldered responsibility for all the financial and intellectual adventures of publishing to be coddled and managed now like a small child even if the woman who did the coddling and managing was as devoted and charming as Ginevra. For the first time Basil wondered if she was exaggerating the state of his heart for some reason of her own . . .

If it had deteriorated to such a degree that his wife was afraid to let him walk alone through the woods for a little while, he was hardly likely to have engaged in such a stressful activity as murder. It was a sort of medical alibi. For that very reason it wakened in Basil the lightly sleeping suspicion of all those who deal with criminals for any length of time. Could all this talk of heart disease be a clever bit of misdirection? Better check with Alcott's doctor. . . .

"What about me?" Swayne asked Marriott.

"Try the road to the village."

"I already did."

"Try again. They might be coming back that way after going somewhere else. I'm going back to the Radanine house now to see if they've doubled back there."

"What shall I do?" asked Basil. "Vanya's mother hardly needs my attention now. Mrs. Swayne is with her."

"Why don't you take a look at the woods near this house? They just might be somewhere close and there's no one here who would notice. Mrs. Crowe is upstairs, but she's asleep."

"Thanks," said Basil.

"For what?"

"For giving me the place where I think they are most likely to be found. There are a lot of questions I'd like to ask those two."

"You think they might stick around this house because it's the least likely place for us to look?"

"That's one reason."

"There's another?"

"Wouldn't you have found them by now unless they are either far away or hiding? I believe they are more likely to have a hiding place in or near this house than anywhere else."

"Why not at the Radanine house?"

"It's a modern house. Privacy is hated in this age of togetherness. Half the rooms in modern houses never have any doors at all, and there are no real nooks and crannies. You could never play hide and seek in them efficiently. But there are almost always good hiding places in old houses."

"But why hide?" demanded Marriott.

"That's one of the questions I'd like to ask them."

"Let's be off," said Swayne. "I'm going to climb the hill at the back of the house. It'll save me about a mile if I don't have to go around to the east side of the road by the

161

driveway."

"I'll take the west side of the road myself," said Marriott. "I can reach that most easily by the driveway."

As he moved away, Basil looked at Swayne. "I'm going to start by having a word with the cook. She may know more about this house than anyone else. Is she in the kitchen?"

"At this hour you'll find her in her own quarters over the garage. She always takes a coffee break before luncheon."

Swayne moved away toward the corner of the house. Even without snowshoes, he didn't make a sound in the deep snow. Once he had disappeared around the corner, the stillness was so lonely that, for a moment, Basil wanted to whistle or stamp his feet, just to destroy that eerie feeling of being watched by something unseen that always haunts unbroken stillness.

Yet he knew that what he needed most now was silence, the mother of reflection. During the last twenty-four hours enforced intimacies with strangers had been distracting to the point of irritation. Impressions of events had been superimposed upon one another as rapidly and incoherently as a *montage* in a movie. Only alone and in silence might he begin to see each event separately and the pattern formed by relationships among them.

His own feet made no sound on the packed snow as he went down the path to the garage savoring the pure, cold mountain air. He no longer wanted sound. To break such silence now seemed to him as if it would be a desecration. In the wilds winter and silence are synonymous unless there is wind. Today there was no wind at all, and if there were any hardy birds or animals abroad, they made no sound in the soft pile of powdery snow.

The garage was a converted stable built at about the same time as the house. Double doors stood open revealing old box stalls and three modern cars, each with a New York license.

The Lincoln was the Alcotts'. Roomy and steady, Basil had found it an ideal car for an invalid when he drove Gisela to the hospital. The Rover convertible looked like Swayne's taste—compact, maneuverable, with luxurious appointments —real leather, real wood. That left the Dodge Dart for the Crowes, a sound, reliable, all-purpose car, but the interior of this one was untidy. Bits of used paper tissue on the front seat, a crumbled newspaper, half a pack of cigarettes. Crowe had been either naturally untidy or very busy.

You could tell a lot about a man from his car. The books on his shelves and the pictures on his walls might be wedding presents or heirlooms. He might furnish his house to please his decorator, he might dress to please his wife or children, but his car and everything about it was his own choice. It told you what he thought about money and machinery, safety and taste, order and cleanliness. It even told you the kind of impression he wanted to make on other people.

An expensive car? Either he cared about machinery or he accepted Veblen's theory that conspicuous waste is the only source of distinction. A well-kept car with a little of the romantic elegance of a carriage? A sense of history, cultivated tastes and some feminine influence. A car with nothing to distinguish it from a hundred thousand others? Either he had no taste or his mind was on something more important than cars. No seat belts? Reckless. A seat belt for the driver's seat and none for the passengers in back? Selfish. What fun Sherlock would have had with cars. . . .

At one side of the building a ramp led up to what may have once been a carriage house. Farther along a narrow door led through an old tackroom to a stairway freshly painted white with a bell in the wall beside it. At the top Basil saw a closed door. He rang the bell and heard a quick step overhead.

Martha opened the door at the top of the stairs.

"I'm sorry to bother you while you're resting," said Basil. "But it's important. I'm looking for Miss Lucinda and the Radanine boy."

"Oh, that boy!" Just as Vittoria had automatically defended her boy and condemned the girl, Martha was automatically defending her girl and condemning the boy. Lucinda was much more Martha's girl than Folly's.

"I've got coffee made," Martha was saying.

"Thanks, I'd like some." Basil went up the stair and came out in a large cheerful room, jonquil yellow and white like the kitchen.

"They did it all up for me." Martha's eyes followed his approving glance with a smile. "Used to be a hayloft."

"They?"

"Mr. and Mrs. Swayne. Everything had to be done over when they took this place. Cream and sugar?"

The hot, sweet, creamy coffee was welcome after the cold outside.

"How long has Miss Skipper been missing?"

"Miss Skipper?"

"That was my name for Miss Lucinda when she was a little thing and I was left alone with her after her mother died. I used to say: 'This house is a ship, you're the skipper, and I'm the crew.' Not this house, of course. The one we used to have in Westchester. She loved being skipper. . . . Has she been gone long?"

"No one has actually seen her since early this morning, but she's probably in the neighborhood with the boy who's missing, too. You've known her a long time?"

"Since she was born. I knew her mother before she was born."

"Do you think she might be hiding just for mischief? And, if she is, where are we most likely to find her?"

Martha was silent. Her skin was the dark brown of West

Africa and her face was West African, too, a face that might have been carved out of some dark, hard wood like ebony or teak. The brow was high, the nose straight, the nostrils and everted lips chiseled sharply and cleanly. The chin was stronger than usual in women either black or white. She bore herself with an air of enduring calm.

"If I knew, you think I'd tell?"

"Not in ordinary circumstances, but these circumstances aren't ordinary."

"She might be in danger?"

"She might."

"I don't know anything. I can only guess."

"What's your guess?"

"Try the house. Miss Skipper has a hiding place there. I don't know just where, but it's somewhere in the house."

"What makes you think so?"

"Yesterday afternoon I looked in every room for her and I couldn't find her. I decided she must be outdoors. Then two minutes after I gave up looking, she popped into the kitchen. She hadn't been out. Her cheeks weren't pink with cold. And she hadn't been far. If she had, she couldn't have got back that fast."

"Is there an attic?"

"Mrs. Swayne says there's just a crawl space, but the roof is pretty high for that."

"You're suggesting that the Crowes kept the attic a secret from their tenants?"

"Either that or the old Miss Crowe who just died kept it a secret from her heirs."

"There are no windows above the upper floor."

"Couldn't there be skylights? From the ground you wouldn't see them among all those gables."

"Odd you should think of all this when Mrs. Swayne didn't."

"Not so odd." Martha smiled. "The woman who cleans the house is the one who knows the house best. I'm the one they come to when something's lost in the house and they want it found."

"There's one other thing I'd like to ask you, since you've known Miss Lucinda so long. Is there any particular reason for her hostility to her stepmother? Or is it just that— traditional resentment of a stepmother?"

The last of the smile faded from Martha's eyes and lips. Now her face looked more than ever as if it had been carved in hard, dark wood. She hesitated, weighing her words, and then spoke reluctantly. "It may be her father's fault."

"Her father? I thought he wasn't even aware there was hostility."

"Perhaps he isn't. Or perhaps he sort of likes the idea of two women competing for him. Some men do. But I think everything would have been different if he had managed things a little more gradually. For several years after Miss Lucinda's mother died she was the centre of his life, and then suddenly she was just nowhere . . . You see what I mean?"

"Yes, I see what you mean. These situations demand tact, and tact is just another word for love." Basil rose.

Martha was putting on her snow boots. "Don't wait for me. I'll be up at the house in a minute and help you look. . . ."

As Basil walked back up the steep path to the house, he came to a break in the trees where he could see other mountains in the distance. Where he stood, each branch and twig of each leafless tree was starkly articulated in the chill, clean sunlight, but the distant mountains faded into a pearly haze that had no apparent connection with the earth.

The mountaintops themselves were rounded because they were among the oldest mountains in the world, Permian, and their peaks had worn away long ago. They had been old before life appeared and to them the two million years of man's existence would seem brief as a summer day.

Now they seemed to float between heaven and earth, dreamlike, enigmatic, fateful. The Abode of the Gods . . .

With a little shiver, he went on.

At the door of the living room he paused. The room seemed empty, yet he had an odd feeling he was not alone. He felt something so different in the quality of the silence that he called out: "Anybody here?"

No answer. The sound of his voice died away, leaving the silence unflawed yet somehow ominous.

He walked across the living room, his footfalls loud as they fell on the parquet between two old Turkish rugs. The silence was thick and heavy all around him. He paused again at the door into the hall and again he had that uncomfortable sense of an unseen watcher observing him. Yet his eyes and his reason told him that he was alone in the room.

That was why he was quite unprepared for the sudden breaking of the silence when it came.

"Do as I do, Mr. Splitfoot!"

15

THE VOICE WAS HARSH as the abrasive sound of a nutmeg grater. Each syllable had a rough edge and there was no inflection or expression.

Was it these peculiarities that made it so hard to tell where the voice came from? Basil had no feeling that it was trying to capture his attention. It was everywhere and nowhere, because it was addressed to no one. A truly inhuman voice.

He turned slowly from left to right, looking all around the room—front door, study door, hall door, dining-room door, terrace door. No one to be seen, and five doors. Wasn't there a Chinese belief that a room with five doors is always haunted?

Now he was facing that dark end of the room farthest from the windows, when a movement caught his eye.

In the shadows, against the gray stone of the chimney piece, there was a vivid flash of turquoise. The croaking voice spoke again: "Pretty-bird! Do-as-I-do!"

Tobermory sidled up and down the chimney shelf, in the manner of the parrot tribe, with his head in one side. The one small, black eye that was visible was fixed on Basil's face with no more friendliness than a shoe button.

"Pretty-bird!" He made one word of two and there was such a total absence of human cadence that you had to listen carefully to understand anything he was saying. It took Basil back to the Second World War, where he had learned to receive International code at military speed. You couldn't hear dits and dahs separately, only the cadences they made with each word. You had to do consciously the same thing you did unconsciously when anyone was speaking—listen for the cadence, not separate words or syllables and when you had to guess, go by context. That quite unconscious process was the only thing that made rapid speech possible. It was because that process had not yet been established that people learning a new language always said to the natives: "Don't talk so fast!"

But now, as Basil tried to understand the bird, the normal listening process was impossible, for there was no cadence and no rational context. He had to listen for words and syllables only. After a few moments he began to acquire the knack. It was then that the bird fell silent.

Would his speech be stimulated by questions?

"So you know about Mr. Splitfoot, Tobermory?"

"No-Frank . . . I-don't-think-so . . . oh-dear-oh-dear . . . toobroo-toobroo-toobroo . . ."

Was it *to brood?* Or *Tobruk?* Or something altogether different?

"Tobermory, if only you would speak a little more distinctly . . ."

"Oh-yeah?"

This was one of those accidentally apposite responses that made so many people sure parakeets understood what they were saying.

Basil sighed. "If only you could think as well as talk! You are the one witness who was actually near Crowe when he died, the only witness present. The fact that you can talk, but not intelligently enough to tell us what happened, makes you quite infuriating."

"Ha-ha-ha!" Then came a blur of syllables so run together and so totally without enunciation that Basil could not distinguish words at all.

"Come on, Tobermory! You can do better than that. Slowly now, and clearly."

Again the response was startlingly apposite.

"Okay-what . . . ?   Soldier-of-the-legion . . . lay-dying-in-Algiers . . ."

"Not really appropriate."

"Oh-yeah?"

Basil winced. "That's enough, Sir Echo. Or shall I call you Mr. Splitfoot? There's something diabolical about you. I wonder how you got out of your cage?"

The parakeet laughed raucously, and that was apposite, too.

The empty cage stood on the centre table, the door open, the wire that had latched it, dangling. Some birds were clever enough to unfasten their own cage doors. Basil had no way of knowing if Tobermory was that clever. Should he try to return the bird to the cage?

He took two steps forward. There was a panic flutter of wings. A turquoise rocket shot up to the chandelier far beyond human reach. Tobermory laughed again.

"All right. Whoever feeds you will have to coax you back into your cage."

The lower hall was dark. The upper hall was even darker. Only one window there. Would it be worth the effort to search this upper floor? Better take a quick look around before trying to find the entrance to the attic . . . if there was an attic.

Basil started with the haunted room at the head of the stairs. The police had left it locked. Hardly likely that

170

Lucinda and Vanya could have got hold of a key.

He moved on to Folly's room. Light with many windows, charming, old furniture all in exquisite order and therefore totally uninteresting from a police point of view.

Swayne's room, half bedroom, half study, was just as orderly and uninformative. A working writer's study with typewriter, filing cabinet and tape recorder. Might be an idea to borrow the tape recorder and record some of the indistinguishable words the bird had been saying. Played more slowly than normal, the meaning might be revealed. . . .

Lucinda's room, on the other side of the hall, was smaller than either of her parents' rooms and furnished a little preciously in a scheme of cream-color, almond-green and pale pink, all borrowed from the colors in a Marie Laurencin print above the bed. Folly's taste, not Lucinda's. Would it have been better to let Lucinda have one room that expressed her own taste, however unformed?

Next came the guest rooms. This must be the Alcotts'. Who else would have heavy pigskin bags today? Only people who had a chauffeur to carry them whenever they wanted one and who didn't care how much they had to pay for excess weight on planes. No wonder leather was being used for suits and skirts these days. . . .

One more guest room. He hesitated before its door. Mrs. Crowe had come upstairs to rest, but she might be awake by this time and she might have heard something if Lucinda and Vanya were on this floor.

He tapped lightly on the door, so lightly that if she were still asleep the sound would hardly waken her.

No answer.

He tried another tap just a little louder.

Still no answer.

Either she was sleeping or she had wakened and gone out while he was with Martha.

Suddenly it seemed important to know which. Gently he eased the door open a little way.

The room was dim, for dark window shades were drawn down three quarters of the way. The windows were open a few inches at the bottom for air.

The bed was in the centre of the room, its headboard against the wall on his right—a double bed with a vast Victorian headboard of mahogany. Serena Crowe lay facing the windows, her back to the doorway where Basil stood. She had pulled a claret-colored satin quilt up to her neck. Her blonde hair was tumbled on the pillows. Her shoes were neatly aligned beside the bed.

Only as he turned back toward the door did it come to him that there was something unnatural in her stillness.

He walked over to the foot of the bed where he could see her face. Sunlight filtered into the room through the narrow slits below the lowered shades. It was unkind to the scars left by plastic surgery, yet there were so many scars he was sure that without surgery her face would have been something she would have had to keep veiled from the world. Even the closed eyelids showed tiny threads of scar tissue and there were more all around the parted lips.

What a bond it must have been—that disfigurement inflicted upon her inadvertently. A bond that would hold Crowe to her irrevocably as long as they both lived.

Basil almost turned toward the door, then hesitated again. What was wrong?

Sometimes you can't see the slow, gentle motion of a human breast in sleep, but usually you can.

He went back to the bed.

The moment he touched her hand, he knew that she had been dead for an hour or so. There is no other cold like that.

172

16

THE SKY HAD DARKENED rapidly after sunset. Now it was the deep sapphire that comes just before the stars appear and man-made lights turn it black. Each living-room window was a jeweled panel in a shadowy wall.

Basil had come into the room to talk to Gisela on the telephone. She had called to say that she was able to leave the hospital now. It was a long conversation, for he wanted to give her some idea of all that had taken place at Crow's Flight since she left. As he talked, dusk had seeped into the room. It was only when he put down the telephone and looked at the windows that he realized how near it was to night.

His gaze came to rest on the Swedish angel chimes on the centre table beside him. The four little candles had burned down to their sockets, leaving a thin film of melted wax on the brass plate where the candleholders stood. He touched the propeller blades of the little fan lightly with one finger. As they moved, they took the four attached cherubs with them, swinging gently in a full circle, but so slowly that the tiny brass rods dangling from each cherub barely flicked the two bells below in passing, making the faintest, farthest, most fairylike of tinkles.

Basil was thinking of what Gisela had just said: "Don't you remember? It was the Christmas we got new chimes and they wouldn't work when we lighted the candles, and we were so disappointed."

"I remember vaguely," he had answered. "It's so long ago."

"It was only yesterday. Little Gisela was five. You took the chimes back to the shop on Christmas Eve."

Silently he had marveled at woman's memory for detail, especially her memory for detail on sentimental occasions. Gisela was like the Boston verse-maker who wrote:

> *"My mind lets go a thousand things*
> *Like dates of wars and deaths of kings. . . ."*

But she could still remember what happened the Christmas when little Gisela was five.

"The man showed you how the little steel point on which the whole thing revolves must be filed absolutely smooth to make it work. Don't you remember now? He took a nail file and with a few strokes removed a burr so tiny it was almost invisible. Then the whole thing worked perfectly."

"Wouldn't oil have helped?"

"I doubt it. He didn't say anything about oil, but he did say the metal must be as smooth as glass and the whole thing balanced exactly if it's to respond to such a slight initial impulse as the updraught from the little candle flames. Is this important?"

"I'm beginning to think so."

"Then you know who . . . ?"

"I'm afraid I do."

"Afraid?"

"It's not going to be pleasant. It never is. Wouldn't it be wiser if you stayed in the hospital a few more days?"

"You know how I hate hospitals and you know how expensive they are. I don't have to go back to Crow's Flight. You can drop me at the ski lodge. We still have reservations, don't we?"

"Yes."

"Are the police still at Crow's Flight?"

"There's a man on guard. After we found Serena Crowe's body, Marriott asked a few preliminary questions and then went to the hospital to discuss both deaths with the pathologist there. He thinks Mrs. Crowe and her husband died the same way and he wants to establish medical evidence for that as soon as he can. He should be back here at any moment."

Basil had sighed as he put down the telephone. The skiing holiday was out of the question now with Gisela's ankle in a cast and the holiday mood disintegrating. As soon as he could get her out of the hospital, they would go back to New York. They had planned to fly to Switzerland and spend New Year's Eve with little Gisela near her school in Lugano. Perhaps they could get an earlier flight . . .

The telephone rang.

Before he picked it up, he switched on the lamp beside it. Immediately the sapphire sky beyond the windows turned black.

"Dr. Willing? Marriott here. Is it all right to talk?"

"There is no telephone extension here, so no one can hear what you say."

"What about your end? Where is everybody now?"

"Folly—Mrs. Swayne—took Mrs. Radanine home some time ago. Swayne and the Alcotts are upstairs. Miss Lucinda and Vanya are in the dining room. The cook is in the kitchen."

"I've got autopsy reports on both crimes now."

"So they were both crimes? I'm not really surprised. I've had the feeling that Crowe's death was murder all along and of course there was no question of it when his wife died so

175

soon afterward, even though there were no apparent signs of violence on either body. Was she pregnant?"

"Yes, but that really doesn't help us much. We're still wondering what caused the nausea. Pregnancy? Or pregnancy plus shock? It could be either."

Basil thought about the notes Cyril Jones had made of Marriott's interview with Serena Crowe. "Until then she didn't seem to be having a difficult pregnancy. It didn't occur to me that she was pregnant, and I'm a doctor. I have a feeling that to get such a visceral reaction from her, you would need a really big shock."

"Such as?"

"Well . . . suppose that something was said during that interview that gave Mrs. Crowe a sudden insight into who had murdered Crowe and why. Suppose that insight indicated that the murderer had the same motive for murdering her. That would be a real shock. Fear like that can cause vomiting."

"If she was that frightened, wouldn't she have appealed to us for protection?"

"Perhaps her greed was greater than her fear."

"Blackmail?"

"Genteel blackmail. Not put into words. She would just see to it that the murderer knew that she had protected him by withholding information and leave the rest to his sense of self-preservation without a word spoken on either side."

"But his self-preservation was more ruthless than she realized, so she was killed instead of paid off?"

"Probably. How was she killed?"

"The weapon looks more like a coarse needle than anything else. It's steel, about six inches long, with a sharp point at one end and broken off at the other. The cross section of the shaft is paler than the rest, as if the exterior metal of the rest were old and tarnished."

176

"How was it used?"

"Do you remember the New York medical examiner's discussion of President Kennedy's death? One thing he said was that the head of a dead man must be examined in detail to find wounds that may not be immediately apparent and that the hair must be combed all over the head to make sure no concealed wounds will escape notice. In country districts autopsies are not always so thorough, but we've been thorough this time. These needles were both sunk into the head at the base of the skull, piercing the medulla oblongata. If there were handles, they were missing, probably broken off short. The ends of the shafts were flush with the scalp and completely concealed by the hair. Her hair was long, as you'll remember, and his wasn't short or close-cropped at all, especially on the neck. If we hadn't had a complete autopsy with thorough examination of the head, such wounds might have escaped notice altogether.

"His hair was thick and a little longer than usual with most men of his age. Her hair was long, worn either in a braid coiled around her head or in a knot at the back of her neck. . . . Is there any sign of those kids yet?"

Sometimes it seemed to Basil that the word "kid" was overworked today, especially when it was applied to adolescents who found themselves in difficult situations. It was curious how few adults realized that such a familiar and patronizing word robbed the young of dignity and self-respect at the very age when both were needed desperately to develop a sense of responsibility. And that word "kid" was subtly permissive. You could overlook behavior in kids that you wouldn't tolerate in boys and girls, let alone young men and young women.

After all, a kid was simply a young goat. Would middle-aged men enjoy it if the young referred to them constantly without any apparent humorous intention as old goats?

177

Basil realized only too well that his view was contrary to the spirit of an age which welcomed familiarity promiscuously in any form. It would never occur to Captain Marriott that there was any other way to refer to anyone under twenty-one.

This was no time to protest, but Basil did avoid using the word himself when he answered.

"We found them in the attic."

"The attic! I didn't know there was one."

"Neither did anyone else apparently. Crowe may have known because the house belonged to his family and he may have told his wife, but the Swaynes say he never told them, and I'm inclined to believe them."

"Why?"

"If they had known about the attic, wouldn't they have searched there when Lucinda was missing?"

"I suppose they would. What were the kids doing in the attic? And how did they find out about it?"

"I was just going to ask them when you called."

"Okay, go ahead and see what you can get out of them. I'll be along as soon as I can."

"I may not be here when you get back this evening. My wife wants to leave the hospital and I'm going to pick her up in a few moments. I'm dropping her at the ski lodge. Then I'll come back here to see you. I should be back in a couple of hours. . . ."

Lucinda and Vanya sat at one end of the long dining table together. A green-shaded lamp threw a spotlight on the playing cards scattered across the satiny mahogany surface and left the rest of the room so nearly dark that the sky beyond the windows here still looked blue rather than black.

Basil had entered unobserved. He paused a moment enjoying the picture of two young heads, one so dark, one so pale, bent together in the circle of lamplight with everything else lost in the shadows beyond them like a Rembrandt painting.

"You're sure you remember the card you picked?" Lucinda was saying.

"Oh, yes, it's the—"

"Don't tell me! That would spoil the trick. I'm not supposed to know what card it is."

"But you do?"

A giggle. "My clairvoyant powers . . . Oh, here's Dr. Willing."

"Don't let me interrupt." Basil drew up a chair.

"It's an old trick Daddy taught me," said Lucinda. "You probably know it already."

"I do indeed." Basil smiled. "It was old when I was a young man in the Navy. But go on. Let's see if you know all the refinements."

She didn't. After five minutes, Basil said: "The first time you go through the pack you must pass the card you know he picked."

"Why?"

"That's when you give the audience a chance to double their bets. They think you missed that card because you didn't recognize it. They think the trick is failing. It never occurs to them that you are so diabolical that you miss that card deliberately, knowing that if you do, they'll double their bets. As soon as they have, you say: 'I'll just go through the pack once more . . .' And that time of course you pause trimphantly and say: 'Here's the card you picked. How did I miss it that first time?' "

"You must have won a lot of bets when you were in the Navy," said Vanya.

"Not at first. I was the sucker who lost until someone let me in on the secret."

"It's all misdirection and bluff, isn't it?" said Lucinda. "Like poker and sleight of hand and—"

"And murder," said Basil quietly.

Lucinda dropped a card, recovered it. Vanya took the pack from her and began to reshuffle it. Lucinda sat still as if she were afraid to speak.

Vanya set the pack down on the table with a little snap and threw himself back in his chair. "Are you accusing us?"

"No," said Basil. "Not of murder."

"Of something else?"

"Of concealing some evidence and falsifying other evidence. Those are serious charges. Why did you write that silly letter and leave it where the police were sure to find it?"

Vanya and Lucinda looked at each other. It was Lucinda who spoke.

"Are you going to tell the police?"

"It will be better for you if I do. It won't do either of you the slightest good to get off with a thing like that scot-free."

Vanya cut the deck, drew a card and turned it over. It was the Queen of Spades. "Ugh!" Hastily he thrust it back into the pack and shuffled again.

"I'm waiting for an answer to my question," said Basil.

"We were trying to help, really." Lucinda sighed. "I suppose you won't believe this, but we were. You see I'd overheard a conversation the afternoon before David Crowe was killed. A conversation between him and his wife."

"You were in the attic?"

"Yes. It was the first time I'd been there. I knew Vanya had a hiding place, but he wouldn't tell me where it was. I was in the upper hall that afternoon sort of looking around for it and I was lucky. I found it. Vanya hadn't said anything about the eavesdropping part of it. He didn't know about that because he'd only been in the attic when the house was empty. So it was a real surprise when I heard the voices."

"You're sure it was David Crowe and his wife?"

"Oh, yes. I've known them for years and I'd have known

180

their voices anywhere. Quite distinctive, you know. His sort of round and resonant and hers nasal and whiny. They were speaking quite loud. He was angry and jealous. He practically accused her of having a lover. I heard the whole thing and then, when he was killed, I realized that no one else knew anything about that situation, except Mrs. Crowe, and she wasn't going to talk about it for obvious reasons. Yet it might have a lot to do with his murder. At the very least, it gave her motive. I didn't think the police would pay much attention if I just told them about it. I kind of hated to admit to them that I'd been eavesdropping and I didn't want to tell them or anyone else about the attic. If it were no longer a secret, Vanya and I couldn't use it as a hiding place any more.

"So I told Vanya and he had this marvelous idea. Instead of just telling the police, why didn't we write a love letter and leave it where the police would find it? They'd have to question everybody about a love affair. We thought, since Mrs. Crowe was guilty, she'd break down under questioning and tell the police all about her love affair. Only she didn't."

"The guilty don't always confess."

"I suppose not, but I was surprised when I overheard her telling the police so calmly that she loved her husband and he loved her and they had a beautiful relationship and she never even thought about another man after she married him, when all the time I knew—"

"You overheard all this when you were in the attic this morning?"

"Yes, and I was shocked!"

Basil smiled. "Suppose she was telling the truth?"

"But how could that be? I heard Crowe accusing her."

"And you heard her denying his accusation. Suppose she was telling the truth then?"

"But then what made him so jealous?"

"That's an important point."

181

They waited for Basil to elaborate, but he didn't.

"How did you guess we wrote that letter?" asked Vanya.

"Guess?"

"Well—deduce. . . ."

"The letter was immature, almost burlesque. Of all the people here, only you two could possibly have written it. When I realized that Mrs. Crowe was probably not involved in any love affair—"

"She wasn't? How did you find out?"

"Let's say I guessed it. The fact that the letter was left where the police were sure to find it was significant. It suggested a clumsy attempt to incriminate someone with forged evidence. Who would do such a thing so clumsily but the very young?"

"We didn't want to incriminate her," insisted Lucinda. "We didn't think she'd murdered anybody. We weren't even sure there'd been a murder then. But we did think that the situation between Mrs. Crowe and her husband might have something to do with his death and that the police ought to know about it."

Vanya was watching Basil's face. "You don't think our letter had anything to do with her death, do you?"

"No, she would have died anyway. But let this be a warning to both of you. It might have had something to do with her death. Don't play with murder, ever."

"So it was murder?"

"Yes. We have the weapons now. Needle-sharp lengths of fine steel thrust into the head at the base of the skull under the hair, silent and quick."

"They were both killed?"

"And by human agency. You can forget all about death from shock and Mr. Splitfoot. He exists, but he's not disembodied. He's in human shape with human attributes, and he's a murderer. I hope I've convinced you of that. It's important that you should not conceal evidence any longer."

"What makes you think we are?"

"Aren't you?" Basil tossed the little ivory elephant on the table. "Do you know what that is?"

There was a whistle of indrawn breath from Lucinda. "I think I know. It's the head of a hatpin, isn't it? There were a lot of old-fashioned hatpins in a trunk in the attic with various handles. I remember ivory elephants. There should be two. They were all in pairs."

"There were. Two murders and two weapons. Each time the little elephant was broken off short under the victim's hair, so the weapon might have escaped notice altogether if the autopsy had not been so thorough. This ivory elephant was found in the fireplace in this room where the murderer must've tossed it, hoping it would not be noticed with the ashes and other debris in the fireplace. An ivory elephant is just the sort of fancy ornament ladies indulged themselves in before 1914, when they wore big hats on top of high coiffures and had to pin the hats in place. I am quite sure that when Captain Marriott gets here with the steel shaft found in Crowe's body we will find that the broken end of the shaft fits the tiny rusted hole in the elephant's side.

"The police found the elephant in the fireplace the morning after Crowe died. The muderer may have hoped it would burn. Even if it didn't, there was a good chance it would escape notice in the ashes and other debris there. No murderer can risk being caught with evidence like that on his person. If something must be disposed of quickly, a fire is the logical place. But there should have been something else there. I looked for it in the ashes when the police found the elephant, but it wasn't there. I think one of you two had found it already and removed it. Inexperience often apes nerve. People with more experience than you two would have been afraid to keep quiet about a thing like that. Where is it?"

Still they hesitated.

"Oh, really!" said Basil impatiently. "I can tell you what it is. A piece of thin, flexible metal with a hole in it and possibly a screw to match."

"Well, I'll be—" Vanya dug down into his hip pocket and dredged up two small objects and tossed them on the table.

"How did you know?" Vanya no longer used the word guess.

"There had to be some explanation for Mr. Splitfoot."

"And this explains him?"

"Partly. A piece of it is missing, a plastic piece that probably melted in the fire or turned into a shapeless blob that was unrecognizable."

"What is it?"

"A clicker. Haven't you ever been in one of those large city hotels where size and efficiency are more important than style or comfort? Haven't you noticed that once you've registered, the clerk summons a bellboy to take your bags by making a sharp castanet sound with one hand? It's louder than a snap of the fingers and not quite so loud as a bell and much more distinctive in a lobby where telephone bells are ringing most of the time. It's loud enough to attract attention without being loud enough to disturb anyone. Some, like this one, are made of flexible metal fixed with a screw inside a sort of plastic cap, so small it can easily lie hidden in the palm of a man's hand.

"I thought of it when I remembered that Mr. Splitfoot's raps had had a castanet sound. Those raps had to be made by someone in the living room. Vanya was at home, as his telephone call proved, and there was no one else in any other part of the house except Martha in the kitchen, and so she

184

was too far away to make the raps.

"How could such sounds be made in full view of everyone else without any apparent movement on the part of anyone? A clicker was the only way. It was small enough to be palmed, and invisible while it was being used. The only movement needed was a slight contraction of one hand, which would not show. It would most likely be tossed into the fire afterward when no one was looking to make sure that it wouldn't be found on the person who used it in case Crowe's death did not pass for a natural death and there was a search for a weapon as soon as his body was found."

"But . . . but . . ." Lucinda was gasping. "The sound did seem to come from outside the room. Don't you remember?"

"Of course. Nothing is harder to determine than the direction of a sound when there is no visual clue to it. Only this afternoon I was startled by Tobermory's voice and I had no idea where it was coming from because I couldn't see him. This is something that has been tested many times in psychological laboratories. The night we heard Mr. Splitfoot, the idea was already planted in our minds that the sound was not coming from among us, and there was no visual clue to contradict this. We couldn't have seen a hand move as slightly as this hand must have moved. So we all felt the sound was coming from outside the room or at least outside our own group."

"Then it was all planned?" said Lucinda.

"Not all of it. Some of it was swift and brilliant improvisation by an opportunist who seized upon any raw material at hand the way some birds will weave any chance met thread or string into the texture of a nest."

"Are you going to tell us who it is?"

"What makes you think I know? I've told you a little of what was done and how it was done, but I haven't said that I know who did it or why."

"Do you know?"

"I can guess, as you would put it, but I may be wrong. You can't expect me to tell you until I'm sure. Why don't you ask Martha to get you something to eat now?"

"I'm not hungry," said Lucinda.

"I am!" Vanya rose with alacrity.

"I don't want to bother Martha if no one else is eating," objected Lucinda.

"We don't have to bother her," retorted Vanya. "We can make sandwiches ourselves."

Lucinda managed a rather pale smile. "You know something that has always bothered me? In books, especially mystery stories? When the author's forgotten what time it is and suddenly realizes that his characters haven't eaten anything for hours, he sets them all to making sandwiches or 'cutting' sandwiches if it's an English book, but the author never tells you what kind of sandwiches and I always want to know. Cucumber or chicken or what? I get to wondering so much about the kind of sandwiches that I lose the thread of the story. What sort of sandwich would people have in the middle of a crisis? Something very French and fancy like creamed *foie gras* on *pain au lait?* Or just ham on rye?"

"How about a club sandwich?" said Vanya.

"Oh, all right. Isn't it odd how the word sandwich all by itself suggests something rare and delectable, but the moment you specify what kind of sandwich it seems commonplace and uninteresting."

"No sandwich is uninteresting if you're as hungry as I am now," said Vanya. "I said club sandwich because it's the heartiest."

"But it means we'll have to go to all the trouble of cooking bacon."

"I'll do that if you're too lazy."

They had reached the swing door into the pantry when Lucinda paused. "Dr. Willing, there's a lot you haven't explained yet. Suppose the raps were made by a slicker and suppose David Crowe was stabbed at the base of the skull with a hatpin, you still haven't explained how or why he rang that bell upstairs just before he died when all the other men were downstairs. Are you going to say that they mistook the direction of sound a second time? That the sound didn't come from upstairs where Crowe was?"

"No, I shan't say that because I'm convinced that it did come from the haunted room where Crowe was."

"Can you tell us how?"

"I've already told you more than I should. Run along and get your sandwiches."

Lucinda went on through the swing door. As it swung back, Vanya stopped it and looked at Basil penetratingly.

"You're making things easy for Lucinda, aren't you? Is this going to be rough on her at the end?"

"Probably. If you can think of any way of getting her over to your mother's house, do so. If not, stay with her and stay close to Martha."

17

BASIL DIALED the number of the garage in Catskill. "Is my car ready?"

"Been ready half an hour. You can pick it up any time now."

Next he called the garage in the village. "I would like a taxi to drive to Catskill so I can pick up my own car there. . . . Yes, I understand I'll have to pay for the trip over though I'm coming back in my own car—"

"Dr. Willing! You mustn't!" The door to the hall burst open and Folly flowed into the room. "I'll drive you to Catskill."

"I couldn't think of putting you to all that trouble."

"No trouble at all. When you get your own car, you can follow me back here. It's so easy to get lost on those mountain roads after dark, as you found out the other night."

"I'll never hear the end of that, will I?"

"It's a tricky road. I'll show you a short cut from Crowe's Clove to this house."

"But I hadn't planned to come back to this house," said Basil. "I thought it would be better for everyone if Gisela and I went on to the ski lodge tonight. If the police want me, you can tell them where we are. I'm sure you understand."

"Then I'll show you the way to the ski lodge. My car's white and easy to follow after dark. Do me good to get out of the house for a while. I'm getting claustrophobia here. Let me talk to those taxi people."

She reached for the telephone and Basil surrendered it. "Mr. Gregg? Never mind this call. I'll be driving Dr. Willing. That's all right. Good night. . . . You want to go now?"

"The sooner the better."

"Just wait till I get my coat."

She came back enveloped in oatmeal tweed lined with beaver. There was a hood that protected her head and framed her face in the soft brown fur. Boots of supple brown leather that looked Italian came up to her knees. She was drawing on fleece-lined gloves to match.

At the door she flipped a switch and floodlights shone on the path to the garage. Basil followed her into the numbing cold of a winter night in the mountains. Always aware of ancient hills, and even more ancient stars above the hills, a human being could not help feeling uncomfortably small and temporary in this landscape.

"I'll back the car out."

Her voice only emphasized surrounding stillness as the floodlights emphasized surrounding darkness. Basil waited ankle-deep in snow as she backed the car out of the garage and halted it. He got into the seat beside her. The car backed and turned and he heard the jingle of tire chains.

"You think chains better than snow tires?"

"Up here I use both! Chains for a snowfall like this. Snow tires for ordinary weather. It won't be bad once we get to the county road."

"It was well plowed and sanded this morning."

"After today's sun a little snow may have melted and refrozen as ice after sunset. The only place you really have to watch is that corkscrew pass over the mountain where you have cliffs rising on one side and a bottomless pit on the other for several miles."

"Well do I remember it! That's where Gisela and I went astray in the fog. It's hard to realize that was only the night before last. I feel as if I'd been here a year."

"I'm sure you do. Summer people often ask in the village if there's any other way they can get back to town, just so they don't have to take that road again. Of course people up here who have learned to drive in the mountains think this is absolutely silly. They're always laughing a little grimly about summer people who 'go off the mountain' when they drive and drink at the same time."

"I've noticed it's always 'the mountain,' never 'the mountains.' "

"That's the series of ridges you have to cross in order to get here, the bastion that protected them until the Thruway brought cars and buses. If you were fighting an old-fashioned battle here, without any air power, you could hold this whole region as long as you held that pass."

She drove on in silence until the lights of the village in the valley rolled into view. "Do you think we'll ever know who killed David and Serena?"

"I hope so."

"Do you?"

"Don't you?"

She sighed. "No. I'd rather not know. It's obvious now that it can't have been an outsider. It has to be someone in our small circle."

"I should think that would be an additional reason for wanting to know."

"Oh, I understand what you mean. You think it's unpleasant—perhaps even dangerous—knowing one of your intimates is a murderer, and not knowing which one. And it is. But isn't it even worse to know if they are people you care about? All these people are strangers to you, of course, so you can't possibly care about them or really understand how I feel."

"I admit that," he answered her. "But surely you can't think it safe to leave at large a person who has killed twice?"

"You're right, of course, but . . ." She sighed. "I expect the situation that led to David's murder was an unique situation that would never arise again."

"And Serena's murder?"

"Arose out of David's."

Did she know or suspect who the murderer was? Basil's mind went back over what she had been saying. Did she really think his attitude unfeeling? Or was she merely invoking the twentieth-century convention that always allots more sympathy to the perpetrator of an outrage than its victim?

It was quite fascinating to see how the convention ran through almost all contemporary literature. In a novel the trick was to start with one of those black and white situations where the old-fashioned reader would automatically identify with the victim. Say the torture murder of a child of three by a man of forty or fifty. The trick was then to show with the greatest psychological ingenuity and deployment of literary art that it was really all the fault of the three-year-old child who was exploiting or corrupting or teasing the poor forty-year-old man, that he was the one who should command the sympathy of all sophisticated readers, that what looks like white is usually black, and vice versa. It was the trademark of the era—inverted sentimentality as mechanical as the senti-

191

mentality from which it derived. It had nothing to do with life as most people lived it, and therefore nothing to do with art.

When Basil tried to put some of this into words, Folly disagreed. "I know what you mean, but I don't believe that what I feel now is inverted corn. It's purely selfish. I don't want to live through an experience that would be so unpleasant for me as finding out that someone I know and like and trust is capable of killing and must suffer for it."

"Purely selfish?"

"Purely. I'm not thinking of the victim or the murderer now. I'm thinking of me. Perhaps the real victim of a murder is not the killer or the killed, but the innocent bystander who has to go on living and pick up the pieces when they've played out their little melodrama."

"That I will not dispute."

"Murderers should think before they murder."

"Murderers don't think. If they did, they wouldn't murder. Nothing is worth the risk they take."

She didn't answer and he looked at her, wondering how much she knew or suspected of what was going on in his own mind at the moment. Her eyes were intent on the road. She couldn't drive and return his gaze. He could take all the time he wanted to study the classic line of that Hellenic mask.

Now they were beyond the village of Crowe's Clove, rounding the hairpin bends that took them down one mountainside and up the next and on across a plateau to the crossroads where they picked up the road to Catskill.

"You really needn't wait for me," said Basil as they drew near the garage. "I'm sure I can find my way back."

"I'd rather wait," insisted Folly. "It would be really awkward if you got lost again tonight with Mrs. Willing wearing a cast."

They were coming to the outskirts of the little Hudson

192

River town. Folly turned and turned again, picking her way easily through one-way streets that were familiar to her and not to Basil. As he saw how confusing the intricate web was after dark, he was glad that she had brought him and glad that she would be waiting for him to lead him back out of town.

He saw his own car under a floodlight in the parking lot of the garage across the street from the hospital. Folly parked her car beside it while he went into the office to pay his bill.

When he came out, she was standing beside her car. "I've got some traveling rugs in the back seat. Will you need them?"

"No, Gisela will be warmly dressed."

She fell into step beside him. "You may need help with her if she's unused to crutches."

Gisela was dressed and waiting in her room. She looked so well and cheerful that the heavy white cast thickening her right leg grotesquely didn't seem to be a part of her at all and neither did the crutches beside her.

"Why, Mrs. Swayne, how nice of you to come!"

"It's good to see you looking so much better. Can you manage those crutches?"

"Oh, yes, but I wonder if I really need them."

"Better be on the safe side tonight. There's ice on the surface of the snow and this is no time for a second fall."

Basil turned to Folly. "Why don't you stay with her and help her downstairs while I bring my car around to the hospital entrance? Then we'll wait in the car while you get yours."

Getting into the driving seat of his own car again made him feel as if he were being welcomed by an old friend after a long absence. He made a U-turn and parked in front of the hospital. Before he could get out of the car, Gisela was coming down the steps. She was using only one crutch. Folly held her other arm and carried the second crutch for her.

Slowly, gingerly, they negotiated the icy steps and pave-
ment. Basil got out of the car and opened the door. A nurse
followed Gisela with her suitcase. Gisela eased herself into
the seat beside the driver's without aid, then swung both legs
around so she faced the windshield.

"Neatly done." Basil smiled. "Now you're safe in the car, I
shan't worry about you any more."

The nurse stowed the suitcase and crutches in the back of
the car.

Folly said: "My car's still across the street in the parking
lot. If you'll wait here, I'll drive around and get in front of
you."

Basil went to the other side of his car. As he got in beside
Gisela, he touched her cheek lightly with the back of his
hand.

"We're not going back to Crow's Flight. We're going to
the ski lodge."

"Good."

He watched Folly cross the street and unlock her own car.
Interior lights came on as she opened the door and climbed
inside and went out a moment later as she closed the door.
Seconds passed before her headlights came on. Now she was
pulling out into the street, sounding her horn.

At the signal Basil swung his car into the street behind
Folly's.

She was going faster than he liked and he found he had to
concentrate to keep up with her. Following another car, even
by daylight and in good weather, can be a tricky business.
After dark, on icy roads, it wasn't going to be easy. Yet it was
better than attempting to find his way alone through the
network of secondary roads, some marked obscurely and some
not at all.

He had tried to memorize the way as they came into town,

but he hadn't succeeded for, after the first three turns, there were no landmarks he recognized.

As they reached the county road, another car passed him and slipped in between his car and Folly's. One of those eager tailgaters who cannot bear to see a few inches between two cars ahead of them. Luckily this one peeled off at the cross-roads. Basil accelerated, moving closer to Folly's bumper. He wasn't really afraid of losing her. She would be watching him in her rear-view mirror and she would pull over to the side of the road and wait for him if he lost her, but it would be much easier for both of them if she didn't have to do that.

They had been climbing steadily. Now they came to the gate to the real mountains at Palenville. They swung around curve after curve without meeting another car. He slacked his pace a little. There were *No Passing* signs on this corkscrew shelf carved out of the mountainside, so he could afford to keep a safer distance.

They reached the summit of the first mountain and began to descend on the other side to the narrow clove where there was a waterfall in summer. At the very bottom, narrowly imprisoned between two great natural walls, they turned sharply and began to climb once more. The turn-off came sooner than he expected, and everything looked unfamiliar from then on. Evidently Folly's short cut was going to bypass Haines Falls as well as Crowe's Clove and take them to the ski lodge by back roads.

He wondered a little: was she sure these back roads were plowed? She must be sure or she wouldn't have risked taking him this way.

It didn't occur to him then to wonder why she was taking him by a route other than the one they had used coming down, which would also have led them to the ski lodge. Afterward he was going to marvel at this, but at the time he didn't even think of it. Possibly because he was too busy straining to concentrate on those red taillights ahead of him that seemed to flip around each corner just a little too fast for comfortable following. If he did lose her and take a wrong turn here, he would be really lost. Even if she stopped and waited or tried to retrace her way and find him, she might not be able to if he had gone far or taken more than one wrong turn. He didn't want that to happen. The sooner Gisela was safe and snug in a warm bed of her own, the better.

At the very thought of losing Folly, he quickened speed again and closed in on the taillights of the white Rover, but it seemed to quicken, too, and that was a little odd. Was Folly determined to keep a fixed distance between them at all times?

He tapped his horn, but still the other car didn't slacken its pace. Should he pull up beside her as if he were going to pass her and call out, asking her to go a little more slowly? He would better warn her. He tapped his horn again as a signal and set his left blinker to flashing, then pulled over to the left and started to accelerate. To his surprise her left blinker started flashing too, as if she were going to make a left turn, so he was forced to fall back again behind her.

"What is she trying to do?" said Gisela.

"Apparently she's going to make a left turn."

"Is there a left turn here?"

"I don't know. I'm completely lost now."

There was a turn. The Rover took it fast, skidded, slowed, accelerated and went on. This road was narrower than the others. Impossible for one car to pass another here.

"Have we been on this road before?" asked Gisela in a small voice.

"No, Folly's showing us a short cut." Basil's own voice was

colorless. "This seems like a private road, hardly plowed at all. Without these new snow tires, I couldn't make it. . . ."

"A very badly kept private road," said Gisela as they lurched over a bump.

There were sharp curves here, too. The Rover's taillights flicked aound another curve. As Basil followed it, Gisela gasped.

He took his eyes off the road for an instant to follow her gaze. Involuntarily he slowed.

The ruins of an old stone house that must have burned stood on their left. They were very high and the drop below them was very close. Far, far below, a carpet of lights shimmered on a vast plain. Far, far above, the milky way was an arch of jewels.

"I've heard about this place," said Gisela. "You have a view of five states."

"But why did Folly bring us around this way? Surely not for the view?"

"You'll lose her if you don't hurry."

"I'll lose whoever is driving that car."

"Then it's not Folly?"

"I'm beginning to wonder . . ."

He took the next blind curve slowly. His caution saved his life. The Rover had stopped. It was parked across the road, broadside to his car, like a roadblock. At the speed he had been driving before, he must have smashed into it. As it was, he had to leave the road and plow through snow to avoid a collision. Luckily this side of the mountain was not too exposed to the wind for the snow to be deep. It was in the hollows and valleys that the drifts piled up. Here it was possible to maneuver.

He swerved, giving the other car a wide berth, and started bearing back toward the road, but, as he did so, the other car moved toward him.

At his back there was only the sheer drop and the vision of infinity. Coming toward him, gathering speed, the headlights of the Rover threw their dazzle in his eyes, masking the face of the driver and everything else inside the other car.

He swerved into a wider curve, still bearing toward the road. The Rover swerved, too, following his car as a compass needle follows a magnet. There was no mistake now. It was the purpose of the other driver to force Basil's car over the edge, even at the risk of both cars going over.

If Basil swerved again, the Rover would swerve again and each swerve would bring both nearer to the edge. What a mad fantasy, to fight a duel with cars. Yet, wherever there is murder, there must always be madness . . .

Basil swerved a third time. As the Rover followed, a door opened in its side and something fell out and rolled. A dead body?

Basil couldn't risk swerving any nearer to the edge. There was only one thing to do.

He pulled his steering wheel around until his headlights were focused on the Rover's in a direct confrontation and then stamped on the gas pedal. His car leapt forward like a horse at a touch of the whip. If only he didn't strike a patch of ice and slip . . . If only the other driver would lose his nerve . . .

He did. The sight of another car coming directly at you at full speed will unnerve even a desperate driver. It was the Rover that slowed a little now, for the first time, starting to swerve out and away from the oncoming car. It was the Rover that struck a patch of ice.

It skidded wide with an hysteric squeal of tortured rubber, turned over and burst into flames. It was still flaming as it rolled over and over and dropped into the abyss.

"Oh . . ." Gisela put her hands over her eyes and buried her face against Basil's shoulder. Where only a moment before there had been so much noise, there was now a long silence.

18

THE SKI LODGE WAS something entirely new for the mountain region—the science-fiction school of architecture and decoration. Life was one visual shock after another, rather like *Dr. Caligari,* or some other futuristic film of the twenties, where the trick is to see everything from an unnatural camera angle.

The ceiling of the main room towered to seventy feet. The large windows, kidney-shaped or triangular or rhomboid, were set in unexpected places, at floor or ceiling level rather than eye level, so you couldn't see out. Other windows were bent around a corner to take in parts of two walls like the windshields of some modern cars.

No chairs. Cushions on the floor, Japanese style, and as Western legs weary quickly in such positions, there was a large, sunken place for legs and feet in the middle of the floor described as a "conversation well." The fireplace was a stove, detached from the wall and sitting in the middle of the room. An old-fashioned stovepipe ran up to the ceiling, suggesting fires in the centres of wigwams and other primordial dwellings that had released smoke through a hole in the roof before the inventions of chimneys.

Inevitable as the detached fireplace was the tall tree, a hemlock this time, that stood with its roots in a patch of earth revealed by a hole in the floor and its upper branches passing through another hole in the roof. At one end of the room, a glass wall enclosed an aquarium filled with tropical fish which occasionally displayed cannibalistic and erotic tastes. TV sets, heated swimming pools and sauna baths were scattered at random about this ground floor. Also various bars for cocktails, milk drinks, coffee and tea.

Lights were concealed and their color changed frequently. They were not really bright enough for such wide-open spaces. After dark the huge room seemed twilit. The effect was dreamlike as masses of people with vacant eyes sat sucking their drinks or trudging about aimlessly, like people in a great airport waiting for a plane that never came.

Here there was none of the cozy, alcoholic gaiety of a small ski resort. The management proudly informed you that as many as five thousand people passed through here on one weekend. "Passed through" was the right phrase. You had a feeling that they were all on the way to somewhere else. There was no society here, only little, anonymous groups, who came together, stuck together and looked at other such groups with indifferent eyes, knowing they would never meet again. On the old ocean liners friendships had been formed among strangers. That couldn't happen here, any more than it could on a transatlantic plane. The place was too large, the people were too many and their stay was too brief.

To Basil the place was as impersonal as a subway car or an automat, an intimidating preview of the anonymous world of the future. Kept on the move by world-wide military or industrial duties, the descendants of "wandering food gatherers" would become wandering money gatherers. There would be no inherited homes, no family traditions, no sense of a personal link with history. No one would stay long

201

enough in one place to establish the sense of living in a neighborhood. Everyone would be "passing through" and there would be no neighbors or friends or clubs, no civic spirit or social circles. Nothing between the minuscule individual with his parasitic dependents and the nation-state, so huge that his mind could hardly grasp its structure or function.

In the iron context of such a technology, the little reproductive group of the family would dissolve, unable to compete with the more efficient mass-reproduction methods of the biological laboratory. Humanity would be completely atomized, each in his narrow cell forever laid while still alive, like coral polyps building an island over millions of generations. Would man lose his taste for language as he lost his taste for love and other personal things? Would he end back in the mute, mindless, pre-human world from which he had once struggled with so much difficulty?

Basil was not the only one aware of the impact of this place.

"I feel as if we had paused to refuel at Space Station Number 6,389 on our way to Betelgeuse," said Gisela.

Ginevra Alcott murmured assent. Bradford Alcott contributed one of his weary sighs, and Basil said: "No one could talk here. We'll take you up to our own quarters."

That was a distinct improvement. The sitting room was built to the scale of human life. The wall that faced the mountains was glass, and on a clear night like this, it gave a wide view of stars. There were no phony fireplaces. Just efficient central heating. No conversation wells. Just comfortably padded armchairs and a sofa. No trees growing in the floor. Just a thick, warm, soft carpet from one wall to another. The only absurdities were the vibrating mechanism in the beds that "massaged" you if you put a coin in a slot and the spigot for ice water that was quite unnecessary in a winter climate where tap water came from the pipes ice-cold. They ordered drinks and roast beef sandwiches and sat around a low table meant for drinks only, facing the stars. Ginevra was the first to speak about the things in all their minds. "It may be an awful thing to say . . . it is an awful thing to say . . . but, now I know the whole truth, I'm glad Frank and Folly died as they did."

"Who says you know the whole truth?" drawled Alcott. "There are a lot of things that Dr. Willing hasn't told us."

"I think you ought to tell them," said Gisela.

"There's not much more to tell." Basil pushed away his plate and leaned back in his chair. "It all began when Frank Swayne discovered the attic, just as accidentally as Lucinda and Vanya had discovered it later. Like them, he also found that he could overhear things said in other parts of the house.

"They were probably not the first to discover this property of the attic. Its possibilities as a listening post may have caused all the troubles among the three sisters, Atropos, Clotho and Lachesis, and the young man all three loved. Possibly because of this the last Miss Crowe concealed the existence of the attic from her heir, David Crowe, and so it was unknown to his tenants. She may have wanted to bury the attic and everything in it forever. It probably wouldn't occur to her that the attic might be discovered once more through accident and once more play its familiar role of destruction in Crowe family history.

"For it was by being in the attic and overhearing conversation in the rest of the house that Frank Swayne discovered that his wife, Folly, had a lover, David Crowe.

"Folly was beautiful. Last love is far more passionate than first love. This was Frank Swayne's last love and he knew it."

Ginevra gasped. "But . . . I thought . . ."

"That Serena was unfaithful to Crowe instead of the other

way round? So did I—in the beginning. So did Lucinda and Vanya. How wrong we were! I began to suspect the truth when first Folly and then you, Ginevra, insisted that Crowe had what used to be called 'a roving eye' or 'an eye for beauty.' Once I knew that Crowe had accused his wife of infidelity it seemed strange indeed that the only evidence of philandering was Crowe's own philandering.

"To a psychiatrist that could suggest only one thing—delusional jealousy. It's a common failing of a certain type of human male. He's almost promiscuous to the point of satyriasis but he is a prey to unconscious guilt and, in our jargon, he projects this repressed guilt on his wife. She is the one he sees as unfaithful as if she were a glass in which he could see nothing but his own face.

"Constantly, with or without provocation, he accuses her of infidelity and makes jealous scenes. As a rule she has never heard of delusional jealousy and doesn't know what to make of it. Sometimes she flatters herself that his jealousy is proof of his love for her, but it isn't in this case. Quite the opposite. He hates her because he hates himself in her.

"Delusional jealousy is rarer than it used to be. Today divorce is more common and the compulsive philanderer is more apt to escape from his situation by becoming a divorce repeater, but such escape was not possible in Crowe's case, because he and Serena had what she called 'an ideal relationship.'

"Every time he looked at the little scars of plastic surgery on her face he was reminded of the fact that he owed her something for having destroyed her beauty. His remorse wasn't strong enough to keep him faithful to her, but it was strong enough to make him feel guilty for being unfaithful, and that's all you need to set up delusional jealousy."

"Why did Swayne have to kill Serena?" asked Alcott.

"Because she was beginning to suspect the truth. When she

learned from the police that both Folly and Ginevra had accused Crowe of making advances to them, she realized for the first time that he might have been unfaithful to her. She could have discounted one such story, but it would be hard for her to discount two. She may not have known about delusional jealousy but she would certainly begin to wonder if Crowe's accusing her of infidelity might not have been camouflage for his own infidelity, planned consciously. Once she got that far, she would see that Swayne had one of the oldest motives in the world for killing Crowe. The shock of that realization, and not pregnancy alone, was the cause of her vomiting.

"Swayne realized that. He couldn't let her get any farther in her suspicion. No knowing what evidence against him she might stumble on next. So he slipped back to the house, where she was alone, and killed her while I was talking to Martha."

"Just when did he decide to kill Crowe?" asked Gisela.

"Last night, when Crowe explained why the room at the head of the stairs was never used. Swayne immediately saw that, if Crowe died in that room without apparent external wounds, or other obvious cause, the macabre circumstances might help to conceal a murder. He would know that autopsies in remote country districts are rarely as thorough as those in big cities with well-equipped laboratories. Such a tiny puncture above the hairline would be hard to see without a microscope. It might have escaped notice altogether if he had withdrawn the hatpin. Why didn't he? Probably because he was afraid that, without the hatpin to act as a stopper, a few drops of blood would ooze out and draw attention to the wound. So he simply broke off the handle—gambling that the broken end of the pin itself was so tiny it would not be noticed by a country doctor—and he lost.

"He was in the attic when he overheard Lucinda and

Vanya plotting their poltergeist trick. Remember Lucinda said she thought she heard a noise in the upper hall that afternoon, but when she looked there was no one there? Swayne had just entered the attic.

"He realized immediately that the hiding place Vanya wouldn't reveal to Lucinda was that very attic, and that Vanya was planning to hide there that night when he faked the poltergeist raps. Swayne was already planning to kill Crowe that night while there were other people in the house and suspicion would be scattered among them if there were suspicion.

"He didn't want either of the young people involved, as they were sure to be if they were using his listening post in the attic. They might be suspected of the crime themselves or they might discover something that would lead them to suspect him. There was no knowing what Vanya would overhear if he were in the attic that night.

"It was then Crowe hit on the idea of frightening them away from the attic. He could tell by the way they talked that they half believed in poltergeists, quite enough to be frightened. He thought he could keep them out of the attic permanently if he could make them believe that the rapping sounds they had planned to fake were real after all."

"Browning," said Gisela. *Mr. Sludge, "The Medium."*

"Yes. His idea was to startle Lucinda in the living room and Vanya in the attic by playing the role of Mr. Splitfoot himself by making three raps in response to Lucinda's challenge before Vanya had a chance to do so, using a clicker for the purpose. It would probably have worked that way, especially for poor Vanya, alone in the eerie candlelit attic hearing the poltergeist sounds he had planned to mock coming from an unknown source.

"As luck would have it, the effect was far more dramatic than that original plan. Vanya was kept at home by his mother because of a feverish cold. Lucinda didn't know this. When she heard the poltergeist sounds, she thought Vanya was making them. Then his telephone call from his home immediately afterward told her that he wasn't in the attic and that he couldn't have made them. Who did? No wonder she fainted.

"With Lucinda put to bed under sedation and Vanya kept at home by illness, Swayne thought he had complete freedom to carry out the rest of his plan, but he underestimated the nerve of the young."

"So he did," said Ginevra. "They were both back in the attic next day."

"Together and by daylight, yes. I doubt if either would have gone back alone after dark."

"And the clicker?"

"He threw it on the fire where the plastic part of it was consumed. The metal part that remained was almost impossible to recognize for what it was without some further clue to its identity. I wouldn't have suspected what it was myself if I hadn't been looking for something that would make casta-net sounds. As he had no chance to buy one after he over-heard Lucinda and Vanya talking, he must have found that one in the house. They have various uses. Sometimes they are used as a signal in private theatricals when the curtain must be raised or lowered. The fact that he knew the clicker was available may have given him the idea of faking the polter-geist just as the fact that he saw old-fashioned hatpins in the attic must have given him the idea of a way to kill Crowe. Swayne was an opportunist, an improviser in everything he did.

"The most impressive example of this improvisation is the way he took over the whole situation and manipulated every-body as soon as I suggested I spend the night in the haunted room.

"Drawing lots? That was to make it seem pure chance that Crowe was chosen—something that couldn't be part of a plan for premeditated murder. But Swayne was a man who knew simple card tricks. I saw Lucinda demonstrate one he had taught her to Vanya this afternoon. Swayne would know enough to force the lowest card on Crowe in dealing.

"Taking a bell upstairs? This was a device adapted from an old ghost story to make us believe that Crowe was still alive an hour after all three of us, including his murderer, had left him alone upstairs."

"And he wasn't?"

"No."

"Then when did he die?"

"When a man is found dead in a locked room—"

"The room wasn't locked," said Alcott. "The door was left open so we could hear the bell. Remember?"

"When I said 'a locked room' I meant a room that no one but the dead man could have entered before his death. No one could have gone upstairs to the room where Crowe was without our seeing and hearing him. The hall door was open so we could hear the bell if it rang and we had the stairs in full view all the time. No one could have come down the upper hall to that room without our hearing something. There is no carpet, only scatter rugs, and the floorboards creak. No one could approach the house from outside without leaving tracks in the new-fallen snow. There were none when the police arrived. No one could have scuffled with Crowe in the haunted room without leaving some marks on the dust in the floor. To all intents and purposes, it was a locked room even though the door stood open.

"When you are absolutely convinced that no one could have entered a room after a man has been left alone in it, there are only two ways to explain his death after he was left alone. Either he was killed by the last person to leave the

208

room or by the first person to come back to it and discover him apparently dead."

"I was the first person to come back to Crowe." There was wonder in Alcott's voice. "Did you suspect me?"

"For a while. But Swayne was the last person to leave Crowe, and it was Swayne who killed him then."

"How?"

"When we left the room, I was at the door and you were halfway to the door while Swayne was still near Crowe. Swayne even touched Crowe and we both saw it. You told the police that Swayne 'clapped' Crowe on the back. I told them he had a hand on Crowe's shoulder. That hand concealed the hatpin. He stabbed Crowe in the back of the neck and snapped off the little ivory handle that was lightly attached to the pin with glue. The tiny wound was hidden by Crowe's hair. The poltergeist incident and the story of the haunted room had prepared us psychologically for the idea of an inexplicable death. But even then there were indications of the truth.

"Any deep puncture of the medulla oblongata causes almost instant death. Crowe couldn't rise or cry out. He just slumped in his chair, eyes down as if he were still looking at the open book on his knee. But as he exhaled his last breath, he had a flash of realization and he summoned enough of his waning will and intelligence to make that last breath a little more articulate than a sigh or a moan.

"You realize now what it was he said under his breath? Tobermory gave us the clue in his own slurred language. Not *Tobruk*. Not *to brood*. That was another of Swayne's improvisations designed to lead us away from the truth. Neither makes sense, but what Crowe said does make sense when you realize that they were old friends and Crowe knew suddenly that he had been stabbed."

"And that was?"

"Isn't it obvious? *Et tu, Brute.*"

"Two things are still unexplained," said Ginevra. "How did Swayne make that bell ring upstairs with Crowe dead and the rest of you downstairs? And why did Crowe accuse his wife of infidelity?"

"Haven't you guessed how the bell was rung? Don't you remember how carefully he hung the bell on picture wire from a picture hook? Don't you realize that the bell was hanging above the open register that pierced the ceiling of the living room and the floor of the haunted room above it? And that that register was near the living-room fireplace? Don't you remember how Swayne threw a big log on the fire just before we heard the bell? The fire was almost dead until he cast the log on it. Then came a sudden burst of flame.

"He used the same principle as the Swedish angel chimes. Hot air rising from an open flame causes a draught. That sudden burst of flame created an updraught strong enough to stir the carefully balanced bells on their wire and jangle them more than once. It created a perfect illusion that Crowe was alive and ringing the bells."

"Jealousy is madness," said Gisela. "He killed Serena and Folly as well as Crowe. He even tried to kill you and me. He was running amuck."

"There is an element of running amuck in all murders. The taboo against shedding the blood of a member of your own clan is as old and powerful as the taboo against incest. You cannot violate either without being pursued by Furies."

"Had he no other motive for trying to kill you?"

"Oh, he had a motive of sorts. He was in the attic when I was telling Lucinda and Vanya how the clicker was used to fake the poltergeist raps. He knew I'd be on to the rest of it soon and tell the police. So he hid in the back of Folly's car under the travel rugs there. Of course she didn't know he was there.

"Remember, Gisela, how we watched her go over to her car and get in? Remember how, just after she got in and closed the door, the interior lights went off and the headlights were a little slow in coming on? During those few seconds, when the car was in darkness, Swayne rose from the back seat, knocked her out cold, put her under the rugs, where he'd been hiding, and drove off himself. We never saw clearly the face of the driver when we were following that car. We were behind it and the interior lights did not come on again. How could we see that it was Swayne, and not Folly? But it was he, and not poor Folly, who deliberately drove us to that cliffside, hoping he could use his car to force our car over the cliff to our deaths."

"Didn't he know that in such a duel he and Folly were likely to be killed as well as you and me?"

"I think he knew, but, by that time, he no longer cared. Folly had destroyed his happiness and he had destroyed himself."